The Meteor Man

D0378198

THE METEOR MAN

A novelization by Cliff Thompson
Based on the original screenplay by Robert Townsend

SCHOLASTIC INC.
New York Toronto London Auckland Sydney

METRO-GOLDWYN-MAYER PRESENTS A TINSEL TOWNSEND PRODUCTION A FILM BY ROBERT TOWNSEND

ROBERT TOWNSEND "THE METEOR MAN" BILL COSBY · MARLA GIBBS · EDDIE GRIFFIN · ROBERT GUILLAUME · JAMES EARL JONES AND ANOTHER BAD CREATION SPECIAL APPEARANCE LUTHER VANDROSS
SINEAD · NAUGHTY BY NATURE · CYPRESS HILL AND BIG DADDY KANE SPECIAL VISUAL EFFECTS INDUSTRIAL LIGHT & MAGIC PRODUCED BY TOBY CORBETT EDITED BY ADAM BERNARD DIRECTED BY JOHN A. ALONZO A.S.C.
PRODUCED BY LORETHA C. JONES WRITTEN AND DIRECTED BY ROBERT TOWNSEND

READ THE SCHOLASTIC BOOK   1993 METRO-GOLDWYN-MAYER INC. ALL RIGHTS RESERVED.

ISBN 0-590-47300-X

12 11 10 9 8 7 6 5 4 3 2 1   3 4 5 6 7 8/9

Printed in the U.S.A.   01

First Scholastic printing, March 1993

Prologue

In the vast, endless blackness of outer space, there would seem to be so much room that things wouldn't collide. But sometimes they do anyway! A long time ago, in a faraway corner of the universe, two asteroids moved toward each other. The first one was as large as a mountain and as green and shiny as an emerald. It drifted slowly past stars and planets, as if it were wandering lost. But the second asteroid, almost as big as the first one, moved like a missile. When the two collided, the big, slow, green asteroid broke apart like glass. Pieces of it went hurtling in all directions — some of them shooting toward our galaxy, the Milky Way. These green, glowing hunks of rock traveled years and years through space, and every second they got a little closer to Earth. . . .

Chapter 1

Beeeeeeeeeeeeeeeeep! Beeeeeeeeeeeeeeeeep!

It was quarter to seven in the morning, and Jefferson Reed's alarm clock brought him out of a deep sleep. The dark brown fingers of his left hand reached out slowly to turn off the alarm; his other hand rubbed his eyes. More asleep than awake, Jeff got out of bed and stretched his long arms. All around him, on the white walls, there were posters of the great jazz musicians Charlie "Bird" Parker, Miles Davis, John Coltrane, and Duke Ellington. Jeff dreamed of being like those men. He played the bass; he and his friends had a band called The Georgetown Three, and sometimes they played in

3

clubs around Washington, D.C., where they lived. But they hadn't hit the big time yet, so during the day, Jeff was still a teacher — and right now it was time to go to school.

Rounding the corner of his bed, Jeff nearly walked into his dog, Ellington. Still only half awake, Jeff reached down and gently ruffled Ellington's floppy ears. " 'Morning, Ellington," he said. And then he continued sleepily to the bathroom.

When Jeff left his apartment and walked out into the hall, an old song was coming from nearby: "Them There Eyes," by the blues singer Billie Holliday. Jeff smiled to himself; he knew the song was coming from Mr. Moses' apartment. Jeff walked down the wooden stairway, holding Ellington by his leash, and stopped in front of his neighbor's open door.

Inside, Mr. Moses sat in his living room in front of a mirror. He was sixty years old, nearly twice Jeff's age — but he tried to act younger. As Jeff looked in, Mr. Moses was wearing a shiny blue sweatsuit, singing along with Billie Holliday, and trying on different toupees.

"Good morning, Mr. Moses," Jeff said.

Mr. Moses was so excited that he didn't even say good morning. Instead, he pointed to his toupee and said, "What do you think?"

Jeff tried to smile, but it turned into more of a frown. The toupee was big and bushy and fake-looking. It was like some kind of small dog; Jeff almost expected it to start barking. "Well . . ." he said.

Grinning widely, Mr. Moses took off the first toupee and put on another. "What about this one?"

He had gone from bad to worse. This one looked like a pile of black spinach. Still frowning, Jeff said, "Well . . . they look . . ."

"Great, don't they?" said Mr. Moses.

When in doubt, change the subject, Jeff thought. He grinned suddenly and said, "Billie Holliday. This music!" Jeff really did admire Mr. Moses' music collection. His walls had shelves filled with all kinds of rare and classic records. "Mr. Moses, let's make a trade," Jeff suggested. "You give me your original Billie Holliday and Duke Ellington records and I'll give you the best of Wynton Marsalis and Diane Reeves."

Mr. Moses laughed out loud. "Never! I

5

wouldn't give my records up for anything in this world. It'd be like cutting off one of my *hands*."

With that, he went back to trying on his toupees. Jeff smiled, and he and Ellington went down the next flight of stairs. At the bottom, sweeping, was Mrs. Walker. She was Jeff's landlady; a friendly, down-to-earth woman, she was about the same age as Jeff's mother. Jeff stopped in front of Mrs. Walker and handed her Ellington's leash. She took it happily, and said, "Thanks again for the tickets tonight."

"No, thank *you*," Jeff told her. "When the Georgetown Three makes it big, and I win an award, I'm gonna say a special thanks to Mrs. Walker, who let me slide on the rent when I didn't have it, who walked my dog and even did my laundry." Holding up his hand, as if there were an award in it, Jeff said, "This Grammy is for you."

Chuckling, Mrs. Walker waved her hand and said, "Bye, Jeff."

Farther down the hall, Jeff came to the apartment of Mrs. Harris, the neighborhood rumor mill. Mrs. Harris's mouth had been compared to many things. (Jeff's personal favorite was "a track star who can't find the finish line. Just keeps on running."). In the time it took the average person to say "Hi," she could spit out three bits of custom-made gossip. (Four, when she was feeling good.) This morning, she was already on the telephone.

Jeff smiled to himself and shook his head. He liked his neighbors — even Mrs. Harris. Seeing them in the mornings and afternoons made his apartment feel like a home. As he left his building and walked to school, passing through the dangerous streets of southeast Washington, he was glad that there was at least someplace friendly to come back to at the end of the day.

Today, Jeff had to be at school early — he was the choir director, and this was one of the mornings they rehearsed. When he walked into the large auditorium, his singers were already there: second graders, eighth graders, and everything in between. No one seeing them for the first time would've known they had come here to sing. Some of the boys were slap-boxing each other, and others were chasing, or being chased by, the girls. But then one of the boys yelled, "Here comes Mr. Reed!" — and all the playing stopped. Some of the kids ran to their places on the stage, while others, defiant, just walked there, slow and cool.

Jeff walked up on stage and stood in front of them. "Good morning, group."

"Good morning, Mr. Reed."

"Let's work some more on the song from yesterday."

Like two eagles taking to the air in slow motion, Jeff's hands rose. Then they dipped suddenly, and the children began to sing. From the most obedient second grader to the most defiant, these children sounded like angels as they crooned:

> *My country 'tis of thee*
> *Sweet land of liberty*
> *Of thee I sing . . .*

Jeff's arms were working, pulling the sweet harmonies from their throats, merging their voices into one unified sound. Suddenly, with a sweeping motion, Jeff's hands became fists frozen in the air. The children all stopped singing at the exact same instant. Then Jeff clapped his hands with an up-tempo rhythm — and the children sang again and began to sway. *From e-ev'ry-y mouuuuntainside, LET . . .*

While some of the choir held this last note, Jeff pointed to the cool, slow-walking boys in the back row. All together, the boys made sounds with their mouths like rappers. On cue, a cluster of tiny seven-year-old girls sang out, sweet and strong. Now, the song was becoming something the Founding Fathers hadn't dreamed of!

While the other singers were going full throttle, a lanky boy — wearing a Public Enemy T-shirt and a baseball cap with an upturned brim — jumped to center stage. As the seven-year-old girls sang *Freedom! Freedom! Freedom! Freedom!*, the boy started to rap:

> *RING . . . like Martin Luther King!*
> *RING . . . like that Gandhi thing!*
> *RING . . . let the voices SING!*

Jeff's eyes shot toward a younger girl. Instead of singing, this girl was chewing gum. When their eyes met, the girl unhurriedly removed the gum from her mouth and stuck it to the back of her hand. The rest of the choir was turning "My Country

'Tis of Thee" inside out: The front-row singers went at it in four-part harmony; the back-row rappers were sputtering and spitting like crazy; the seven-year-old girls were belting it out like grown women; and Jeff's arms were wild. Just when a listener would've thought it couldn't get any more intense, the gum-chewing girl jumped in. She let out a high, perfect note that brought all the sounds together, from the rappers on up. The choir, now one mighty force, pushed on to the end of the song — and brought it home with perfection.

A smile stretched from one side of Jeff's face to the other. When his second graders sounded like this, he was on top of the world. He felt as if there were nothing he couldn't do.

What he didn't know was, that feeling would soon be put to the test.

Somewhere in space, a green hunk of asteroid moved a few feet closer to Earth.

Chapter 2

After rehearsal, Jeff walked down the hall, making his way past students and other teachers. A second grader had just handed him a note telling him to come see Mrs. Laws — the principal. He had an uneasy feeling. Mrs. Laws was a little like the police: If she wanted to see you, you knew it couldn't be good news. No doubt, Jeff had done something wrong. What could it be this time? Jeff searched his memory, but he couldn't think of much. That didn't mean anything, though. Half the time, when Mrs. Laws started yelling at the top of her lungs and calling Jeff everything but a fried egg, it was for something he thought he'd done *right*. There was no way to tell. Jeff wished Mrs. Laws would just let him teach in peace. Better yet, he wished he didn't have to teach at all. To Jeff, substitute teaching was . . . well, *okay*. He loved directing the choir, of course. But the rest of it? Eh. It would pay the bills until Jeff could play music full-time. That's what he *really* wanted to do. So what if he didn't practice his bass as much as he should? What he lacked in discipline, he knew he made up for in talent. One of these days, The Georgetown Three would take the world by —

Pow! Rounding a corner, he bumped into Michael Anderson. Michael, as always, had on a white lab coat — he was the school's science teacher. More importantly, he was Jeff's best friend, and the manager of The Georgetown Three.

"Whoa," Michael said as they bounced off each other. "How you feel, Jeff? You ready for tonight?"

"You know I am," Jeff said, and they slapped five.

"The first show's already sold out," Michael said. "The second is almost there. But look here — " He reached into the pocket of his lab coat and pulled out a gadget Jeff had never seen before. It was like a cross between a can opener and a UHF antenna. "This device I just invented will monitor the vibrations of the audience — it'll record mood shifts caused by the music. This is a money maker!"

"That's great," Jeff told him, in a voice that really said, *Now I know you're crazy.* "So did that scientific mind of yours remember to bring the tapes to give the record companies?"

"You know I did. I'm your manager — you just keep the music coming from the baddest jazz trio in D.C."

They slapped five again. Then Michael said, "And I got some women lined up for you."

A disgusted look crossed Jeff's face. "Aw, man . . . not this again. I told you I don't want to meet anybody right now."

"Jeff, man, you got to get over Stacy. You broke up four months ago. You got to get on with your life."

"I know, I know . . ."

"Anyway, first show, Debra's bringing her cousin Denise. She's kinda fat but she's got a cute face. Second show, Anita's gonna bring some friend she says is a ten, but without her weave she's a six."

"A six, that's cool," Jeff said, but his mind had gone back to Mrs. Laws. "Look, I gotta go. I just got a note from the Warden — "

"Just appease her," Michael said. "You're not going to be here much longer." Holding up his gadget, he said, "Move over, Wynton Marsalis! I will have it down to a science!"

Stacy. Michael could've talked all day without mentioning her name, and it would've been fine with Jeff. It was bad enough running into her every day; like Jeff, she was a substitute teacher. It had been four months since she'd broken up with him, but seeing her all the time always made it feel like it had just happened. Michael was right, of course: It was time for Jeff to get on with his life. The thing was, though, he missed being with Stacy. She had dumped him because he didn't *appreciate* her enough. He never gave her flowers, and he had failed to get her presents on Christmas *and* her birthday. Of course Jeff appreciated Stacy — it was just that he didn't always have the time or the money to show it. Anyway, it wouldn't have hurt her to be a little more understanding.

But there was time to worry about that later. Right now, Jeff was walking into Mrs. Laws's office.

As he was about to go through the open door, someone was shoved out of it. It was Dre Hawkins, an eight-year-old boy who had been in Jeff's class. Right behind Dre, pushing him and smacking him in the head, was his mother. Trying to duck one of his mother's smacks, Dre ran right into Jeff, and a comic book fell out of his back pocket.

Dre's mother yelled, "Say excuse me, Dre!" and *whap*, she smacked him again.

Dre looked up at Jeff. It was a look of simple, uncut hatred. Jeff was the reason why Dre's mother had come to school — the reason why she was now using his head for a handball. A couple of days before, Dre had started a fight in Jeff's class. Well, he hadn't *really* started it; he had just thrown the first punch. It had started because another boy was teasing Dre about his raggedy clothes. Dre had been in other fights for the same reason. Jeff had thought about calling the parents of the boys who teased Dre. But he didn't have time to talk to all those parents — there was always band rehearsal, or something else going on. But he had to do something, so he called Dre's mother. That was why Dre was now looking up at Jeff with undisguised contempt.

"Didn't you hear me, boy?" Dre's mother asked. "Say excuse me to Mr. Reed!" And she smacked his head *again*.

Looking at the floor now, Dre said very quietly, "Excuse me, Mr. Reed."

"Don't worry about it," Jeff said, feeling a little ashamed. He reached down and picked up the comic book that had fallen out of Dre's pocket. He handed it to Dre and said, "Here you go." But Dre wouldn't accept it.

"Thanks again for calling me, Mr. Reed," Dre's mother said. "If he gets out of line again, I'll be back." And she continued pushing her son through the hall.

Jeff looked at the comic book in his hand — *The Faceless Crusader*. Then he started again into Mrs. Laws's office. But now someone else was coming out, and Jeff bumped into this person, too. Jeff was about to say "Excuse me, I'm sorry" —

but then he saw who it was, and all he could manage to say was, "Stacy."

"Yes, it's me," Stacy said coldly. "Or did you forget I work here, too?"

"I've . . . um . . . been meaning to call you," Jeff stammered.

"What for?" Stacy shot back. "What have we got to talk about?"

Jeff was trying to come up with an answer when Mrs. Laws's secretary spoke. "Mr. Reed, Mrs. Laws is *waiting* for you."

"Coming," Jeff said. He turned to say "I'll see you later" to Stacy. But she was already gone.

When Jeff walked into the office, his spirits — what was left of them — fell. Mrs. Laws was standing in the middle of the floor; her hands were on her hips, her toe was tapping, and her face was the face of a bull who has seen a red cape. One word came to Jeff's mind: *help*.

"You've gone too far this time, Mr. Reed!" Mrs. Laws shouted.

"W-W-What did I do, Mrs. Laws?" Jeff asked.

"Look!" Mrs. Laws said, pointing across the room.

Although he would rather have done almost anything else, Jeff looked. Sitting on the sofa was a thin, middle-aged man. On the other end of the sofa was his wife, who was twice as big and looked madder than a wet hen. Seated between them was their son, Louis Williams. Louis was a skinny nine-year-old boy with thick, black, horn-rimmed glasses and teeth that grew in about nine different directions. Today, his arm was in a sling, his right leg was in a cast, and he had a bandage across his nose.

"What happened to you, Louis?" Jeff asked, horrified.

But it was Mrs. Williams who answered. "You!" she roared at Jeff. "You're the one filling his head up with all this junk. We have taught him to stand up for himself and fight the bullies. But he doesn't listen to *us*. No, he says *Mr. Reed* teaches us different. *Mr. Reed* told us we should run from bullies and *Mr. Reed* tells the smaller kids to practice running, hiding, and eating their lunch fast so nobody will take it!"

"Well . . . I didn't mean *run*," Jeff said. "I meant . . . you know . . . jog a little, maybe . . . or just walk fast . . . because he's so little and the odds are against him. I was just trying to help."

"*Help?*" yelled Mrs. Williams, standing up. "Well, thanks to your help, every bully in this school is beating the living daylights out of Louis! Look at that cast! Look at that sling! A little first-grade girl did this!" Mrs. Williams took a step toward Jeff. "Mr. Reed, have you ever stood up to anybody?"

"Yes," Jeff said, although he couldn't remember when.

"Better yet," Mrs. Williams said, "Has anybody ever taken you and . . ."

"That's enough," Mrs. Laws said, stepping in front of Jeff and probably saving his life. "I'll handle it from here, Mrs. Williams. Mr. Reed, may I remind you that you are just a substitute teacher. No more of this!"

"I was just telling Louis about the reality of how life is," Jeff said.

"I don't care," Mrs. Laws replied. "Teach from the books, not from your sorry philosophy on life. I wish you would spend more time on your lesson plans, and less time on that jazz trio of yours. And another thing — I hear you're changing the arrangement of 'My Country 'Tis of Thee.' Don't you dare change it! I won't have it!"

"But you haven't even heard it!" Jeff said.

"And I don't want to. That's all."

"But . . ."

"That's *all*!"

Jeff left Mrs. Laws's office feeling totally friendless.

Walking home from school that afternoon, Jeff thought, *Misunderstood*. That's what I am. He felt misunderstood by Stacy, Dre, Mrs. Williams, and Mrs. Laws. Of course, when Jeff thought hard about it, he realized that all those people had pretty good reasons for being mad at him. But that wasn't a very pleasant realization — so he thought about something else.

When he got to the block where he lived, he saw a group of familiar faces. Jeff's father was walking down the street with Mr. Moses and Mrs. Walker. They had just been to the store and were carrying home bags of groceries.

"Hi, everybody," Jeff said, catching up to the group.

"Oh, hi, Jeff," they all said pleasantly.

Immediately, Jeff felt better just being in their company. It sure was nice to talk to people who didn't look like they wanted to hit him with something.

But Jeff's good feeling vanished when he glanced down the street. About fifty feet ahead, in the middle of the sidewalk, a drug deal was going down. Money was changing hands between a skinny, strung-out junkie and three men. The three men were dressed alike. All wore expensive designer suits and shiny, leather shoes. Their hair was done in different styles. But their hair had one thing in common: It was all the color of gold. Jeff recognized these men as the Golden Lords — the gang that terrified kids and cops alike, and held southeast Washington in the palm of its hand.

Nervously, Jeff said to his father and neighbors, "Let's cross the street."

But Jeff's father wasn't about to do as his son said. Ted Reed was a feisty man who didn't run from anyone, let alone "two-bit hoods," as he called the Golden Lords. Sometimes, when Jeff compared himself to his father, he wondered if he'd been switched with another baby at birth. "I ain't crossing this street for nobody," Mr. Reed said.

"Dad, come on," Jeff said.

"Ted, don't be crazy," Mr. Moses said.

Mr. Reed looked at him with a disgusted expression. "Are you scared?!"

"Doggone right, I'm scared. I don't have to prove nothing to nobody. If I want to see a hero, I'll go rent *Rambo*."

Mr. Moses, Mrs. Walker, and Jeff all crossed the street. But Mr. Reed kept walking toward the gang.

"Ted!" Mrs. Walker called from across the street.

But it was too late. Mr. Reed had marched right between the junkie and the Golden Lord with the Philly haircut — the one called Goldilocks. Mr. Reed bumped Goldilocks's shoulder, and a drug vial fell to the sidewalk.

Goldilocks looked down at the drug vial; it was unbroken. He smiled at Mr. Reed and said, "You're lucky it didn't break."

"Is that right?" Mr. Reed asked as he crushed the vial with his foot.

Goldilocks moved toward Mr. Reed with the look of a murderer in his eye. But he was pulled back by a second Golden Lord called Uzi. Uzi whispered in his ear. Goldilocks looked around. A police car was driving by slowly. Across the street, Jeff, Mrs. Walker, and Mr. Moses were watching. Mrs. Harris, telephone in hand, was watching from her second-story window.

Goldilocks steadied himself, glared at Mr. Reed, and said ominously, "See you . . . later."

"You see me now! Whatchu gonna do?" Mr. Reed said. Then, seeing the police car, he got louder: "Punk! With your fake blond hair!"

The Golden Lords walked away. Jeff, Mrs. Walker, and Mr. Moses, seeing that the danger had passed, came back across the street. Jeff was full of admiration for his father. He wished *he* had so much courage. Then again, he thought, what would be the use? If you stood up to the Golden Lords, they just crushed you anyway. If that police car hadn't come by, Jeff thought with a chill, his father might be dead now. What was the use of being a hero?

High above, a green hunk of asteroid entered the earth's atmosphere.

Chapter 3

At a little after nine in the evening, Jeff left his apartment again. He was dressed in a baggy, cream-colored linen suit. In one hand he carried his upright bass, which was just as big as he was, and in the other hand was his car tape deck. Jeff was feeling good. The defeats and aggravation of the school day were behind him now; he was on his way to the club to play some music. Not only that — there would be some record company executives in the audience. If they liked what they heard, The Georgetown Three would have it made!

Whistling, Jeff walked up to his white Volkswagen Rabbit and put the bass in the back. Then he climbed in the driver's side, inserted the tape deck, and put his key in the ignition.

From there, Jeff's evening began its downhill journey.

The car wouldn't start. Jeff turned the key again. Nothing. Then he realized why: There wasn't a drop of gas in the tank. He'd have to go to a service station, get a can of gas, and bring it back. Did he have enough money? He looked in his wallet. It was as empty as the gas tank. He sighed and said some words that his mother had spanked him for using when he was little. Well, there was only one thing to do now. He got out of the car, locked the door, and started walking.

Two blocks later, he entered the Community Day Care Center. On the first floor was a big, open room with cinderblock walls, tile floors, and about a hundred folding chairs. About fifteen of the seats were filled, mostly with older people. They were all listening to the speaker at the front of the room — Jeff's father, Ted Reed.

"These gangs take over because people let them," Mr. Reed was saying. "If we challenged them, just maybe they'd think twice. But as it is now, they got us living like animals. Bars on every window, alarms on every car. But now, if we patrol our streets — especially Drake's Place, which everybody knows is the main drug avenue — we can make a difference. And when we patrol, we need to wear these." Mr. Reed reached into a bag and pulled out an orange neon cap with COMMUNITY WATCH on the front. Putting the cap on, he said, "With everybody wearing one of these, the Golden Lords and all those other gangs will know we mean business!"

At that moment, several people began talking at once. Jeff saw his opportunity. Quickly and quietly, he walked up to his father and whispered, "Hey, Dad."

Mr. Reed looked at his son with a surprised expression and said, "Don't you have a show?"

"Yeah, but I ran into a problem. You think you could, um, spare about ten dollars?"

"This is about the third time this month! What you think I am, one of them automatic teller machines?"

Jeff was about to answer, but then Mrs. Walker started speaking. Holding up a whistle, she said, "This will be a signal for anyone that hears it to call the police. This way we can work with the police department — "

Mr. Moses cut her off. He was wearing another of his toupees. The hairs drooped over his forehead like a waterfall. "Are you crazy? I'm sixty-eight years old. I can't even walk that good. And you want me to patrol the streets!"

Mrs. Harris, the neighborhood gossip, joined in. "I agree! And I heard all the gang members in the Golden Lords carry guns. I'm sorry but this is *police business!*"

"You're crazy if you think I'm gonna walk down a dark alley with a loud orange hat on my head and a whistle hanging round my neck," Mr. Moses added. "I can see the headline now: 'Golden Lords kill old man in loud orange hat and stuff a whistle down his throat!'"

Jeff's father looked disgusted. "Ernest, you make me sick playing helpless. When it's time to do something for the community you can barely walk, but I see you don't have no trouble making it to the liquor store every couple days."

"That's none of your business where I go!" Mr. Moses retorted.

Again, a lot of people started talking at once — so many that no one could be heard over anyone else. Jeff spoke to his father again. "Dad, how 'bout that ten dollars? I'm in a jam."

With a "why me?" expression on his face, Mr. Reed pulled out his wallet and gave his son a ten-dollar bill. "You should be coming to these meetings, Jeff. This is your community, too."

"But we can't win, Dad," Jeff said. "There's nothing we can do. We may as well get smart and move out. Well, anyway . . . thanks for the money."

Looking tired, his father sighed. "You're welcome, son. Hope the show goes well."

"Thanks, Dad."

Outside, Jeff sprinted to the service station, got a can of gas, and jogged back to his car.

When he got there, he thought, This can't be happening.

The back window and the driver's side window had been smashed in. His tape deck was gone — and so was his bass. All that was left was a lot of broken glass, sparkling in the night like jewels. Cursing and pulling at his hair, Jeff walked around the car three or four times in a daze.

He came out of the daze when he heard a muffled scream. It seemed to be coming from an alley a few feet away. Hesitantly, Jeff walked toward the alley and peeped around the corner. When he saw what was happening, his heart began beating fast. A teenage boy had his hand over the mouth of a woman and was dragging her backward down the alley. A second boy was searching through the woman's purse.

Jeff searched the ground frantically and finally picked up a beer bottle. Holding it like a weapon, he shouted down the alley, "Let that woman go!"

The two boys looked up with terrified expressions. That was when Jeff recognized them. The boy with the purse was Dre. And the other boy wasn't a boy at all, but a girl. Her nickname was Squirrel, and she was the gum-chewing, sweet-voiced girl in Jeff's choir.

Seeing them, Jeff was so hurt and angry that he forgot his fear. He shouted, louder this time, "I said let her go!"

Squirrel and Dre were as still as parking

meters. For a second, there was complete silence.

But the silence was broken by strange sounds from farther down the alley. The sounds got louder, and Jeff realized they were coming from a group of people. Then the group stepped into the light, right behind Dre and Squirrel. Jeff dropped his beer bottle. There were at least twenty men in the group; they all had on designer suits with the letters *GL* stitched into the lapels, and each one's hair was dyed blond. Yes, it was nighttime, and Jeff Reed, who had never been mistaken for Indiana Jones, was standing in an alley with the Golden Lords.

While his mind was still taking in *that* idea, six Junior Lords appeared. Then came still more Lords — they looked just like the others, from their suits to their hair. Except for one thing: They were all about four feet tall. Jeff had heard about this, but he didn't believe it — until now. These were the Baby Lords. (And one of them was holding Jeff's tape deck!)

Faster than you could say "sitting duck," Jeff took off running, and the Lords took off after him.

All except for one. He was tall and handsome, with eyes colder than January. He wore a long, black coat draped over his shoulders, he played with a Slinky while he watched the chase . . . and when he emerged from the shadows, he held a tiger by its leash. This was Simon Hawkins, the leader of the Golden Lords.

Simon began walking slowly down the alley. When Dre and Squirrel saw him coming, they forgot all about the woman they were robbing, and she ran away screaming.

Standing in front of Dre and Squirrel, Simon said in a deep voice, "This is *your initiation*. You want to be Golden Lords, then *go get him*." Looking at Dre, he added, "And don't think you get no special treatment just 'cause you're my brother."

Dre and Squirrel took off after Jeff.

Meanwhile, Jeff did his imitation of Jesse Owens. His heart was doing some kind of drum solo, and he was sweating in places where he didn't even know he had sweat glands. But this was no time to stop and rest — the Golden Lords were in hot pursuit. They were harder to shake off than a head cold. Jeff ran down streets, up hills, and around corners, but every time he looked back, there were a dozen or more blond heads ten feet behind him.

Then he had an idea. He turned a corner and ran down a narrow alley. The Golden Lords followed, but there was only room for two of them at a time. While they were fighting to get ahead of each other, Jeff put some distance between them and himself. He got to the end of the alley and found himself in front of a tall wire fence. He began to climb. He was halfway up when one of the Lords grabbed his foot. Jeff wiggled free, but lost his shoe in the bargain. He got to the top of the fence, climbed down the other side, then half-ran and half-hopped down another alley.

A few feet away, he saw two trash bins. He did some fast thinking: Should he hide in one of the bins? If he did, and the Lords found him, he would be dead. On the other hand, they were close behind him now — and how much longer could he run from them with one shoe? His decision was made. He ran to one of the trash bins, opened the lid, held his breath, and jumped in.

Through a hole in the bin, Jeff watched

some of the Lords run past him. But then — oh, no — three of them came toward the bins!

Just then, Jeff heard a voice say, "Come on! He wouldn't be that stupid to hide in there!"

Jeff breathed a quiet sigh of relief.

And then someone raised the lid.

Jeff closed his eyes and waited for a gunshot — the last sound he would ever hear. But it didn't come, so he opened his eyes. He found himself looking up at Squirrel.

From down the alley, a voice said, "You see something over there, Squirrel?"

Squirrel was quiet a moment. For the third time that day, Jeff looked in her eyes. He couldn't tell what she was thinking — but what she was thinking would mean either his life or his death. Finally, Squirrel said, "Nah . . . nobody." She slammed the lid back down and darted away.

Thank you thank you thank you, Jeff thought. Through the hole, he watched the remaining Lords run past. He pressed a button on his digital watch, and 10:44 lit up in red.

* * *

Later, still in the trash bin, Jeff pressed the button on his watch again. This time, it read 2:27.

For nearly four hours, he had been hiding in there, sitting on top of garbage and heaven knows what else while his limbs got stiffer by the second. But it was worth it, if it kept him out of sight of the Golden Lords. He guessed they were far away by now, though. He reached up, pushed open the lid, and, grunting, climbed slowly out of the bin.

Jeff was walking down the alley, trying to avoid cutting his unshod foot, when he noticed something very, very strange. The ground all around him was bathed in a soft green light. Then, suddenly, green ashes appeared in the air, falling to the ground like snow. Jeff looked up — and what he saw made him wish he were still being chased by the Golden Lords.

A meteor, huge and bright, bright green, was falling toward him. Jeff ran screaming down the alley. When he looked back, the meteor was even closer — in fact, it almost seemed to be following him, twisting and flaming through the air.

Jeff kept running. To his horror, he came

to a dead end. He turned around, and the meteor was closing in. One second, it entered the alley; the next second, its green light filled his vision; and the next, it smashed into him, crushing him against the wall, burning through his clothes, melting into his skin. The last thing he heard was his own voice, screaming. And then he collapsed, his clothes and body smoking.

A few feet away, a piece of the meteor the size of a soccer ball lay glowing on the ground. Two mutts came running up to it, followed by a man. The man had a patchy, black-and-gray beard, worn-out, stained clothing, and black fingerless gloves. "Now what have we here?" he said as his crusted fingers reached down toward the meteor.

Chapter 4

The thing that woke Jeff up was the sound of someone praying "Heavenly Father," a man's voice said, "please watch over him. I believe everything happens for a reason, so . . . I leave it all in Your hands. . . . Amen."

The voice seemed to be coming from far away. Still, Jeff knew he had heard it before. Who was it? It was on the tip of his tongue. If only he could open his eyes and see . . .

Now there was another voice — this one belonged to a woman. "I'm sorry, sir, you'll have to leave now. Visiting hours are over."

"Listen," the man's voice replied. "I need somebody to talk to. I'm really concerned about *him*. What time do you get off work? I want to discuss his condition."

Jeff could tell that the woman, whoever she was, was good-looking — and the man was trying to get a date. And then he knew who the man was.

"Good *night*," the woman's voice said, firmly.

Jeff opened his eyes just in time to see his friend Michael leave the room. He tried to call him back, but he couldn't speak. Then he saw the woman. She was wearing a nurse's uniform. So he was in the hospital.

The nurse noticed that Jeff's eyes were open and she walked over. He understood why Michael had tried to get a date with her: She was beautiful. "Well, hello there," she said, smiling. "Welcome back to the land of the living. A friend of yours was just here. And your parents just left a little while ago. They were very worried about you. But you're gonna be okay." Taking his pulse, she said, "You're doing much better already, Mr. Reed."

Jeff tried to talk, but failed again.

"Don't try to speak yet," the nurse said.

"You need to rest. If you need anything, just push the button on the side of the bed, and I'll be here. My name is Vanessa and I'm gonna take good care of you . . . okay?"

Jeff managed to nod.

"Would you like me to open your window?" Vanessa asked. "It's a beautiful night. There's a full moon."

Jeff nodded again. Vanessa went to open the window, then said, "There you go, Mr. Reed. If you need anything, just push the button." And then she left.

Jeff stared out the window. It was a full moon, all right; it was big and round and glowing. Jeff tried to figure out why he was in the hospital. The last thing he remembered was being chased by the Golden Lords. Had they caught him and beat him up? Was that why he was here? He kept staring at the moon. Suddenly, the moon's roundness, and the way it glowed, reminded him of something — something terrible. Then he remembered the meteor.

The whole night came flooding back to him: catching Dre and Squirrel robbing the woman, running from the Lords, losing his shoe, hiding in the trash bin, staring up at

Squirrel, and finally, being hit by the meteor. It was all too much. Jeff began to cry. He cried himself back to sleep.

When he woke up again, he was startled. There were about thirty people in his room, packed in like socks in a drawer, and they were all staring at him. There were doctors, nurses, orderlies, and even a few cleaning people, and most of them were holding notepads.

Then one of the doctors, a man with white hair, said, "All right, Nurse. Begin."

A nurse walked over with a pair of scissors and began cutting the bandages off of Jeff's face. When she was finished, the doctor looked at Jeff with a horrified expression, and said, "Oh — oh, *no* — "

Jeff found his voice and said, "Let me have a mirror!"

The nurse handed him one. Jeff looked at his reflection. "This is how I always look."

"Oh," the doctor said.

A young, attractive woman doctor, who was holding a large medical book, spoke up. "I don't understand," she said. "I was here when this man was admitted. He had third-degree burns all over his body. Where are they now?"

"Another case of a patient being diagnosed improperly. In my day, when doctors were more responsible . . . ," the white-haired doctor said haughtily.

The young woman doctor ignored him and walked closer to Jeff. She looked back and forth from Jeff to the book with a confused expression on her face.

She stepped even closer to Jeff. The medical book brushed against his hand. When it did, Jeff saw — did he really see it? — a tiny green spark.

The woman doctor was practically standing in Jeff's face now. "I saw the burns myself, but there's no scar tissue anywhere now. *Why?*" she said.

As if he were speaking to a child, the white-haired doctor said, "A *real* physician might surmise that this is an example of the Stromburg Theory. The severely burned skin tissue has caused the tissue underneath to heal, under the stress of — "

"Wrong!" Jeff yelled.

"I beg your pardon?" said the white-haired doctor.

Jeff told him, "The Stromburg Theory states that *minor* burns, *not* third-degree burns, can heal under stress. Look in the book. Page 294. Third paragraph, middle of the page."

The woman doctor did as Jeff said. She turned to page 294 and read through it quickly. When she looked up again, her face had lost all its color. "He's right!"

"Thank you," Jeff said, cool as a cucumber. He added, speaking to the woman doctor, "And congratulations on your engagement. George must be a nice guy — to write you from Seattle every week."

The doctor looked thoroughly confused. Then she seemed to remember something. She opened the medical book to the back page and pulled out a letter — from her fiancé in Seattle.

Speaking to the whole group, sounding like a seventy-year-old professor, Jeff said, "The Stromburg Theory wouldn't apply to this case, but Heinrich's theory of the skin's ability to reverse scar-tissue damage may be applicable." Glancing at the white-haired doctor, Jeff added, "You, especially, should reread chapter fourteen."

The doctor crossed his arms; his face turned a deep, rich shade of red. "Why chapter fourteen? Please tell us."

"Well," Jeff said, "because in chapter fourteen . . . there's . . . um . . ." Suddenly, Jeff's thought vanished. He completely forgot what he was about to say. "Where was I?" he asked, helplessly.

"Yes. Well," the white-haired doctor said, smiling coldly. "Thank you *very* much for your medical tips, Mr. Reed. I would like to run a few more tests on you, and then you'll be free to go."

He turned to leave the room, followed by the rest of the staff. The last to leave was the young woman doctor, who kept glancing back at Jeff as if he were something she'd never seen before.

That night, Jeff was awakened by the sound of something hitting the floor. He looked to his left. An orderly was bending over to pick up a bedpan and was apologizing to a patient. Relieved, Jeff closed his eyes again. But then they popped back open. He said aloud, "I have a room to myself."

Jeff threw his covers off and got out of bed. He walked toward the patient and the orderly. He stopped when he came to the wall. He put his hand on it; it was solid. But, behind it, *he could still see the patient and the orderly*.

Jeff walked to the window. He looked down at the parking lot. There was a couple sitting in a car — *in their underwear*.

"I'm . . . seeing through things," Jeff whispered.

He thought again about the green spark he saw when the book touched his hand. He thought of how, just for a while, he could remember everything in that book — even the letter tucked in the back.

"What's happened to me?" he whispered.

Chapter 5

"A *meteor*?!" Michael said. He and Jeff were in Michael's convertible. Michael was driving Jeff home from the hospital. "You're trying to tell me you were hit by a *meteor*?"

"That's what I'm trying to tell you."

"Jeff, I teach science. Take it from me — the chance of you getting hit by a meteor is about, oh, one in a billion."

"What else could it have been? How else do you explain something the size of a boulder that fell from the sky and burnt me to a cinder? That's not all, though." Jeff paused. He knew that if he told Michael the rest of it, their next stop might be St. Elizabeth's Mental Hospital. But he had to tell somebody. "Something very, very weird happened last night."

"Your whole accident has been pretty weird," Michael said. "One minute you're burned, the next minute you're not. So what else happened?"

"I realized I could . . ." Jeff swallowed. "I could see through the walls."

Michael just shrugged. "That's just the medication they gave you. The stuff'll have you seeing all kinds of things."

"But I'm telling you — I really could see through things."

"Jeff, did I ever tell you about when I got my wisdom teeth taken out? That stuff they gave me — I thought I could actually read my dentist's *mind*. Okay?"

Jeff thought about it a second. "Maybe you're right," he said. Of course, the medication didn't explain what happened with the medical book — but he thought he'd leave well enough alone.

"You know who was really concerned about you?" Michael asked. "*Stacy*. She asked me how you were every day."

"That don't mean a thing," Jeff said. "She broke up with me, remember? She said the only thing I cared about was my music."

"Oh, speaking of that — when you didn't show up the other night, I canceled the shows, but the crowd wouldn't leave. So I played the demo tapes over the house system. People went crazy! They loved it! Unfortunately, they loved it more than the record executives did. I tried to give them the tapes, but they passed."

Jeff sighed. He was pretty disappointed. "Oh, well."

"I have been talking to another record company though," Michael said. "A smaller one. And I'm looking for a new bass for you."

His bass. With everything else that had happened, Jeff had almost forgotten it had been stolen. Remembering it was like having it stolen all over again. Jeff shook his head and said, "Story of my life."

Meanwhile . . .

On the other side of the city there was a cluster of gray, drab-looking warehouses. But in the middle of the warehouses, blocked from view, was a four-story brick building. In a room on the second floor, the Golden Lords and Junior Lords sat around a long table. Only one of them was standing — their leader, Simon Hawkins. He paced back and forth in front of a map of the east coast cities.

Simon said to the other Lords, "We now run the drug market in D.C., Baltimore, and Philly. At the rate we're going, in three months we'll be ready to make the move on New York City."

Across the room, the telephone rang. Uzi answered it and passed it over to Simon.

"Hello, Mr. Byers," Simon said. "How are you? That's great. The boat gets in tonight? Good. What . . . a present? For me?"

While Simon was still on the phone, the door to the room opened. In walked half a dozen Baby Lords, all wearing sweatsuits and carrying lunch boxes with tigers on them. They put the lunch boxes on the table and opened them, revealing stacks of money.

"Nothing," Simon was saying on the phone. "We're just, uh, having lunch. I do want to talk to you about something, Mr. Byers. I think it's time I took on more responsibilities. New York, for instance." After a pause, he said, "Why is that funny? All right . . . anyway, I'll have someone pick up my present tonight. Thank you, Mr. Byers. Bye."

"Goldilocks, give me a count," Simon said, hanging up the telephone.

Goldilocks escorted the Baby Lords, and the money, out of the room.

"Now," said Simon. "Bring in the new recruits!"

The door opened again. Dre and Squirrel walked in.

One of the Golden Lords led them over to two chairs by the wall and sat them down. Then the rest of the Lords walked over and stood around them, forming a semicircle, with their arms crossed.

"So . . . here are our recruits," Simon said. "The two that think they have what it takes to become Golden Lords. Well, suppose you tell us exactly why we should let you join us." He pointed to Dre and said, "You first!"

"Well . . . I wanna join the Golden Lords because . . . they cool," Dre said nervously.

"We *know we* cool," Uzi said. "We talkin' 'bout *you* now. What can *you* do?"

"I can fight good," Dre replied.

"And who have you fought? Some little

skinny pip-squeaks half your size?" Simon asked him.

"Uh-uh," Dre said. "I fought some big boys."

"And why did you fight them?"

"Cuz they was makin' fun of me," Dre answered. "They always makin' fun of me. Just cuz I ain't got good clothes like they got." Dre struggled to hold back tears. "I wanna be a Golden Lord so I can show 'em I'm as good as they is. I wanna show 'em I'm somebody, too!"

When Jeff walked into his apartment, Ellington jumped all over him. "Heyyyyyy, boy!" Jeff said, grinning and hugging his dog. He hadn't realized how much he'd missed him. Ellington was licking him everywhere. "Sure is good to see you, Ellington!" Jeff said. "Did you miss me? Yeah . . . I know . . . I missed you, too. Hey, you must be hungry. Let's go get something to eat."

They went into the kitchen. Jeff opened the cabinet, where there were several cans of dog food.

"What would you like, Ellington? Liver, chicken, or beefy beef?"

Ellington barked excitedly and wagged his tail. Hearing the words *red can*, Jeff said, "Okay. The red can it is." He took it from the shelf. "That means beefy — "

Jeff froze.

He looked at Ellington, thought for a second, and said, "Nah." He went to find a can opener. But then Ellington barked again, and this time Jeff heard the words, "I'm starving."

Jeff backed up against the wall. "Hold up," he said. "Hooooold up." The meteor and his hallucinations in the hospital were one thing. But thinking that Ellington could talk to him was something else. Still, what if . . .

Jeff suddenly started barking like a dog. As he barked, he thought, If you can understand me, Ellington, nod your head.

Ellington nodded his head.

"I need a drink," Jeff said.

He walked quickly to the refrigerator. When he opened it, the door snapped off its hinges.

A while later, Jeff was sitting on the living room floor, gently scratching Ellington.

Jeff barked, "Do you like it when I scratch you there?"

"No," Ellington barked back. "It hurts."

Jeff thought for a while. Then he barked, "Tell me something. When you go to the bathroom, why do you raise one leg?"

"Well . . ." Ellington replied.

Someone knocked on the door. Jeff answered it, and Michael walked in, carrying Jeff's mail.

"Bills, bills, bills . . . and *Jet* magazine," Michael said. He tossed it all on the table, and then said, "Now tell me why I had to drop what I was doing and rush over here."

"Michael . . . I can talk to Ellington!"

Michael raised one eyebrow and looked sideways. Then he cleared his throat and said, "Jeff, that thing that fell on you in the alley . . . did it hit you anywhere near your head?"

"Man, I'm not lying. Listen." Jeff barked to Ellington, "Say hello to Michael."

"Hello, Michael," Ellington barked back.

"Jeff, this is stupid," Michael said. "You barked and he barked back. So what?"

"I forgot, you can't hear what Ellington's saying. Michael, I'm telling you, something happened to me! How can I prove it to you . . . wait a minute. I know."

Jeff walked back into his living room. Michael followed. Jeff stood behind the couch, looked at Michael, smiled, and said, "Prepare to be convinced, old buddy."

"I'm prepared," Michael said, yawning.

Without another word, Jeff reached underneath the couch with one hand. Then, as if the couch were an empty paper bag, he raised it above his head.

"Well?" he said, still holding it there.

For once in his life, Michael didn't know what to say.

"And that's not all," Jeff said, putting down the couch. "I can touch a book, and for thirty seconds, I'll know everything that's in it. Just by touching it!"

Michael's expression seemed to say, *I must be dreaming.* But he told Jeff, "Okay. I'll get the *Jet* magazine. I know you haven't read that." He got it from the table and said, "Okay. Touch it."

Jeff touched it, and a tiny green spark flew.

Michael flipped through the magazine and stopped at a random page. "Okay. What's on page twenty?"

"People page. Photos. The names Eric Sawyer, Karl W. Taylor."

"You got it," Michael said. "Now. Page thirty-three."

"Society World," Jeff said. "Photo of four couples who just got married."

"Right." Michael flipped to a woman pictured in the centerfold. "I'm looking at the 'Beauty of the Week.' What does she do?"

"She's an actress, a model, a singer, and a dental technician," Jeff said.

"Right. Her measurements?"

"Thirty-six . . . ah . . ." Suddenly, Jeff's mind went blank.

Michael looked at his watch and said, "Sure enough. Thirty seconds." And he added, "You really do have superpowers!"

"Now that we've got *that* straight," Jeff said, "look at *this*." He handed Michael a newspaper. The headline on page two read, "Emerald Meteor Shower in Washington, D.C."

"You *were* hit by a meteor. I can't believe it!" Michael said.

"I know how you feel," Jeff told him.

Meanwhile . . .
A few blocks away, the man with the

patchy beard and worn-out clothes was standing in an alley. He was leaning on a grocery store cart; inside the cart were some old books and a banged-up telescope. The man stared at a brick wall. Through the wall, he could see into someone's living room. A game show was on TV. It was *The Price Is Right*.

A pack of mutts came down the alley toward him.

Marvin barked, "Find any food?"

"Nah," the first dog barked back.

The man frowned.

Another dog barked, "Anything good on TV?"

"Nah," Marvin barked back.

Chapter 6

"I've been thinking," Michael whispered. He and Jeff were in the school cafeteria, standing in line with other teachers who were waiting to order breakfast.

"What have you been thinking?"

"Jeff, you got to use your powers. You got them for a reason."

"What reason?" Jeff whispered.

"For The Georgetown Three! Think about it: In the opening of the show, you could lift up the piano with one hand while Phil plays his solo! People would pay anything to see that!"

"Yeah . . . let me think about it."

Suddenly, Michael was looking at something behind Jeff. His expression was different. "Stacy really looks good these days," he said.

"What?"

"Turn around."

Jeff turned around. Stacy was standing at the back of the line, picking up a tray and utensils. She sure does look good, Jeff thought. There were times when Jeff felt almost sick that he had lost her. She was about the prettiest woman he had ever seen. But it wasn't just that. She had a lot of sense. And she was very sweet — under the right circumstances.

"She hates me," Jeff said.

"She loves you," Michael replied.

"No, she doesn't. Watch." Jeff waved until he got Stacy's attention, and then he motioned for her to come over. To his surprise, she did.

With his heart beating fast, Jeff said to her, "I was wondering if you'd like to join us for breakfast."

"That would be nice," Stacy said. Jeff's spirits soared. And then they were shot down. "My *new boyfriend*, Malik, said I should be more friendly to you since it was over between us."

Stacy got in line ahead of Michael. Michael leaned back and whispered to Jeff, "She hates you."

"I'd like wheat toast and a bowl of oatmeal, please," Stacy told the cook.

Michael told the second cook, "Two eggs over easy and bacon."

Jeff said to the third cook, "Two heads of lettuce and a stalk of broccoli."

"Are you serious?" The cook asked. Stacy and Michael looked around at Jeff, too.

Jeff shrugged. "That's what I've been craving the last couple of days."

When the three of them were seated at a table, Michael asked Stacy, "So what's your new boyfriend like?"

Jeff made a mental note to strangle his friend later.

"Oh, Malik?" Stacy said. "He's so thoughtful — he's always bringing me candy or flowers or some other little present. And he's so *cute*. I always just want to grab him and kiss him and . . ."

Biting into his broccoli, Jeff thought, God, take me now.

* * *

At the end of the day, Jeff was walking down the hall, on the way to a meeting, when he saw Squirrel. "Hey . . . Squirrel," he said. "Come here a minute. I need to talk to you."

Squirrel rolled her eyes, but she followed Jeff over to a corner.

"First, I have to thank you . . . you saved my life the other night," Jeff said.

Squirrel looked up at Jeff a moment, then shrugged.

"But listen," Jeff went on. "Why do you want to be . . . part of the Golden Lords? *Why?* What do you need them for?"

"Because if I join 'em now, when I grow up I'll be important."

"But can't you be important another way? Why do you have to be one of *them*?"

"Because they get the money and the respect," Squirrel said. "Anyway, what else am I gonna be?"

"Are you kidding?" Jeff said, almost yelling. "As well as you sing? You could be a soul singer. Or a gospel star. Or anything you *want* to be! You just have to believe in yourself enough."

"Who says I can do all that?" Squirrel asked.

"Who says you can't?" Jeff replied.

She looked at him a moment, then shrugged again. "I gotta go now, Mr. Reed."

Depressed by his conversation with Squirrel, Jeff walked into the teachers' meeting. He took his seat at the table beside Michael. Then Stacy walked in and sat on the other side of the table, right across from Jeff. As if the situation with Squirrel weren't bad enough, now Jeff had to spend the whole meeting sitting across from Stacy, knowing she had a new boyfriend. Sometimes Jeff didn't know why he bothered getting up in the morning.

"All right, let's begin," Mrs. Laws said. "Mr. Little mentioned to me a problem that he was having. Mr. Little?"

Mr. Little was appropriately named. He was very thin and not much taller than his students. He said, "My problem is Aaron Wood. He won't bring his supplies to class. He sleeps in class. When I woke him up the other day, he used foul language at me."

Michael passed Jeff a note. It said, "I have to tell you about my wild date with

Pam." Jeff smiled — for the first time all day.

Mr. Little continued. "I suspended Aaron from school that day, and that same day, all four tires on my car were slashed. Aaron used foul language again today. I suspended him today, and do you know what he told me? He said, 'I hope you have bus fare!' Which means he plans on slashing my tires *again!*"

"What would you like me to do, Mr. Little?" Mrs. Laws asked.

"I would like to transfer Aaron to someone else's class," he said. "I've done all I can do."

"Well," Mrs. Laws said, "since we are a team, I don't think the transfer will be a problem. Why don't we transfer Aaron to . . ." Her eyes searched the room, and fell on Jeff. "Mr. Reed's class."

Jeff was about to complain, but then he had an idea. He thought of this as a chance to impress Stacy. So he said, "I'll take Aaron. That's fine with me, because I really *care* about these kids."

Mr. Little became defensive. "I care! I do everything I can. But kids like Aaron don't want to learn."

"That's what I hate," Jeff said. "Teachers who don't try. What was that I heard you say over lunch? 'They don't pay me enough to be a teacher *and* a parent?' "

"That's right!" Mr. Little was almost shouting now. "I'm a teacher, not a baby-sitter!"

"True," Jeff said, "but you shouldn't give up. So the parents don't always do their jobs! That's no reason to give up on the kids. It's not their fault." Jeff sneaked a glance at Stacy. She was watching him with new respect, and nodding. Jeff decided to lay it on thick. "I don't care what you say, Mr. Little. Right here in our school we have some of the greatest kids that . . . ever . . ."

Jeff found himself looking through a wall. He could see some kids breaking into a locker and stealing. He looked away.

"If the parents don't get involved," he continued, "then it's up to us . . . to . . . play the . . ."

He could see through another wall. Two kids were spray-painting "Mr. Little is a jerk." He looked away again. This time, his X-ray vision picked up what was happening outside. He saw Mr. Little's car, and there was Aaron Wood, slashing the tires.

Jeff glanced sadly over at Mr. Little. "Do you have bus fare?" Jeff asked. "I mean . . . these kids are not . . . that bad. It's just that . . . they're . . ."

Jeff was too distracted to finish. But Stacy jumped in to help. She said, "I think Jeff's trying to say that these kids are *ours*. And I think he's right. Parents or no parents, as teachers we can't give up on our students!"

"Exactly," Jeff said.

He and Stacy smiled at each other across the room.

After the meeting, Jeff walked home from school with a good feeling.

But when he was two blocks from his apartment, the feeling vanished. He saw his mother, Mr. Moses, and Mrs. Walker helping Mr. Reed out of a car. His father had a bandage on his head, and his arm was in a sling.

"Dad!" Jeff broke into a run. "Daddy! What happened?!" he asked when he caught up to the group.

"Your father thinks he's Superman, that's what," Jeff's mother said. "A little while ago he smart-mouthed his way into a fight with some of the Golden Lords."

"Nobody walks all over me," Mr. Reed said. "I don't care how many there are."

Before Jeff could respond, two BMWs suddenly pulled up. When the doors opened, Goldilocks, Uzi, and three more Golden Lords got out. Slow and cool, they walked up to Jeff and his parents and neighbors.

Goldilocks looked at Mr. Reed and smiled coldly. "Well, well, well," he said. "Back from the hospital already. That was fast." He cracked his knuckles and added, "Now maybe we can finish what we started."

Chapter 7

Goldilocks reached for Mr. Reed's arm. Without thinking, Jeff knocked Goldilocks's hand away, and shouted, "Get your hands off him!"

Goldilocks looked as if someone had just insulted his mother. He and the other Golden Lords surrounded Jeff.

"I meant . . . w-why can't you leave us alone?" Jeff stammered.

One of the Lords, the tallest, meanest-looking one of the bunch, stepped toward Jeff. His face was twisted up in a look that would've scared a bear away. He drew his gigantic arm back and let his fist fly at

Jeff's stomach. Jeff closed his eyes and prepared to die.

But that's not what happened.

Jeff heard a scream, and for a second he thought it had come from him. But when he opened his eyes, he saw the Golden Lord who had just punched him screaming like a newborn baby. His hand, which had just hit Jeff's stomach, was a mangled mess.

Two more Lords rushed at Jeff. Jeff shoved them both away. They went flying — *really* flying. One of them crashed into the side of a parked van. The other landed in the middle of some trash cans across the street.

Up and down the block, doors began opening as neighbors came out to watch. One of the Golden Lords' BMWs backed down the street.

Someone yelled, "Jeff! Look out!"

Jeff looked around and saw the car headed right for him. There was no time to dodge and nowhere to run.

At fifty miles an hour, the car hit Jeff. But Jeff didn't budge. Instead, the car stopped dead. The driver came crashing through the windshield, landing on the sidewalk in a shower of broken glass.

"No seat belt, huh?" Jeff said.

A lot of things began to happen at once. Police sirens were heard in the distance; Goldilocks and Uzi jumped in the second car; the remaining Golden Lords ran for their lives.

From the BMW, Goldilocks called out to Jeff, "I don't know how you did that . . . but you'll be gettin' yours!" With that, the car screeched away.

The crowd that had formed on the sidewalk began to applaud Jeff. Jeff's parents looked at him with their mouths hanging open.

"How . . . how'd you do that?" Mrs. Reed said.

"You on steroids?" Mr. Reed asked.

"No." In a daze, Jeff began walking home. His parents followed. "That accident I had . . . I was hit by a meteor," he told them.

"A *meteor*?" his parents said together.

"Yes. The meteor gave me these powers. Mom, Dad — don't tell anybody, okay? Not yet."

"Son," his mother said, "what difference does it make if we tell anybody or not? The whole neighborhood just *saw* you."

"Make something up," Jeff said. "Tell them it was just adrenaline, or something. Please?"

"If that's how you want it, okay."

When Jeff woke up the next morning, his clock read 9:37. "Oh, man, I'm *late!*" he yelled. He noticed Ellington, who was on the floor near the bed. Jeff barked, "Why didn't you wake me up?"

"I tried," Ellington barked back.

Jeff got in and out of the shower so fast that the water almost didn't touch his body. Getting dressed, he buttoned his shirt up wrong, and almost put his left shoe on his right foot.

"Do you know you're wearing one blue sock and one green . . ." Ellington barked.

"No time to talk now!" Jeff answered. "See you later!" And he ran out of the apartment.

When he had gone a block, he heard a car speeding up behind him. He looked around and saw the BMW from the day before — with a machine gun sticking out the back window.

Jeff tried to run, but before he'd gone

one step, the bullets started flying. Jeff got hit, five, ten, fifteen times. As people nearby shrieked and cried, Jeff hit the ground like a sack of flour. The BMW sped away.

Five seconds later, the car screeched to a stop again. The Golden Lords in the car had seen what the neighborhood people saw: Somehow, Jeff was standing up.

Inside the car, Uzi was yelling, "I don't get it! I hit that dude with everything!" He shoved another ammo clip into the machine gun. "Back this car up!" he said. The car zoomed backward, headed right for Jeff.

Jeff, meanwhile, was standing in the street, dazed. He started flexing his arms. As he did, fifteen bullets popped out and fell on the ground.

He looked up and saw the car coming for him. This brought him out of his daze. He took off running down the street.

The BMW gained on him. Uzi stuck the machine gun out the window and aimed it right at Jeff's head. When Jeff looked back and saw it, he began to run faster. Faster. *Faster —*

The next thing Jeff knew, he was flying!

He went up through the air, out of control, like he'd been shot from a cannon. He flailed his arms wildly, trying to grab hold of something, and managed to grab the arm of a street lamp. He wrapped his arms and legs around it and hung on for dear life.

In the car, Uzi said, "Did he . . . just . . . ?"

"Simon ain't gonna believe this!" Goldilocks replied.

The car sped away.

Still hanging from the street lamp, Jeff said, "What am I doing up here? I'm scared of heights!" Slowly, he began crawling down the arm of the street lamp, toward the pole. Before he made it, one of the bolts holding the arm to the pole popped off — from Jeff's weight. Then another popped off. Jeff looked over and counted: Three bolts left.

Jeff froze. He didn't breathe or blink. The three bolts stayed in place. Well, this is good, he thought. As long as I never have to move again, I'll be just —

Uh-oh. He had to sneeze. He tried to fight it; he twisted his face this way, then that way, then this way again. But the pressure kept building in his nose, until he finally said, "AaaaaAAAAHHHHHH-CHOOOOOOOOOOooooooooo!"

Pop, pop, pop went the three bolts — and Jeff fell, fell, fell. When he hit the street, the sound was like an explosion. He shook his head to clear it, and looked around. He found himself in a hole the size of a ditch. His weight had made a crater in the middle of the street! Climbing out, he saw shattered windows, fallen trees, and people running in every direction. Dogs were barking, and car alarms went off. Trying to go unnoticed, Jeff walked quickly and quietly down the street.

Block after block looked the same. There was broken glass everywhere and people were yelling. Jeff stopped at a brownstone on a corner, went up the steps, and knocked on his parents' apartment door. His father answered it, and the first thing he said was, "Did you feel the earthquake?"

"You could say that," Jeff answered.

He followed his father inside. The TV was on in the living room. The newscaster was saying, "Washington, D.C.'s first earthquake registered three-point-five on the Richter scale. It was felt as far away as Baltimore."

Mr. Reed turned off the TV and said to his son, "Jeff, your momma and me stayed up all last night . . . thinking . . . about your powers."

"That's right, Jeff," his mother said, coming out of the bedroom.

"Mom, Dad, I'm starting to get scared. The gang — the Golden Lords — they're after me now."

Mr. Reed just smiled. "Well, son, if you have powers like them guys in the comic books, you got nothing to worry about. Nothing can penetrate your skin. Bullets, knives, nothing. Right?"

"Well . . . right," Jeff said.

"There you go! Nothing can hurt you! Relax," his father told him, settling back in his easy chair. "We gotta decide what you gonna do first. You could clean up the drug houses, stop the Golden Lords, and avenge me. Then go after the big drug dealers. *Or*, you could go international, and straighten out that mess over there in South Africa."

Jeff was shaking his head. "Dad, you're taking this too far."

"No I'm not." His father smiled mysteriously and said, "And your mother's got a surprise for you." He stood up. "Just close your eyes and follow me."

Jeff sighed, and closed his eyes. His father led him down the hall. They turned a corner. Mr. Reed said, "Okay, son. You can look now."

Jeff opened his eyes. His mother was standing beside her sewing machine, grinning from ear to ear. She was holding up a costume. It was so gaudy that it almost hurt Jeff's eyes. The material was bright green, with silver and gold tinsel lining the sleeves. On the chest were two big M's, made from rhinestones and Mrs. Reed's earrings and necklaces.

"Momma . . . what in the world is *that*?"

"Your uniform," Mrs. Reed said proudly. "You gotta have a uniform to fight crime . . . Meteor Man."

"Meteor . . . *who*?"

"Think about it, Jeff. Why did that meteor hit you?"

"Because I have the world's worst luck?" Jeff said.

"No," his father said. "It was because we need a *real* superhero."

72

"These gangs need a wake-up call," his mother said. "And you've got to have a uniform." Smiling devilishly, imitating a TV announcer, she added, "Because no one must ever know the true identity of Meteor Man!"

"Momma, stop talking like that!"

"The uniform needs a little work, but we'll take care of it," Mr. Reed said.

"Yeah, maybe the tinsel and rhinestones are a bit much," Mrs. Reed said. "I just want you to be the best-dressed superhero. Better than Superman and all the rest!"

"Tuesday, I want you to come by for dinner," Mr. Reed said. "Bring Michael. I'll cook all your favorites. And in the meantime, just think about . . . Meteor Man."

Chapter 8

The Golden Lords' conference room was empty — except for three figures. Uzi and Goldilocks sat in chairs, side by side, looking like two first graders in the principal's office. Standing in front of them was Simon.

"So let me get this straight," Simon said in a calm voice. "You put fifteen bullets in him, and he . . ."

"And he was still standing!" Uzi said.

"It's the truth," Goldilocks added. "And then he . . . flew up that pole. Like he was some kinda superhero."

"Hmmm," Simon said, stroking his chin. "Very interesting. Yes. You shot him and he didn't fall. Maybe he *is* a superhero. On the other hand . . ." A scowl suddenly appeared on Simon's face. "Maybe he was wearing a *bullet-proof vest*! Did you morons ever think of *that*?" he shouted.

"But, Simon — "

"Don't 'but' me! Now tell me what happened again — and this time I don't want any cock-and-bull story about how he *flew up a pole*! If you lost him, say you lost him!"

"But, Simon, that's what we . . ."

"*Shut up!*"

Simon paced back and forth. He seemed to be trying to calm down. "I want to study this character," he said. Then he seemed to have an idea. "Get me two recruits!"

A while later, at the Community Day Care Center . . .

Every seat in the place was filled. Some people were even standing. In the front row, Jeff sat next to his parents. At the front of the room, Mrs. Walker was conducting the meeting.

"Good evening, everybody," she said. "The reason for this special meeting is to thank Jefferson Reed for what he did yesterday. He singlehandedly chased away that gang!"

The crowd burst into applause for Jeff.

Jeff smiled shyly and nodded at the people around him.

Unnoticed, a teenage boy slipped in the door with an instant camera.

Mrs. Walker continued. "Jeff, your mother told us all how you were hit by that meteor and how you've got superhuman powers." The crowd applauded again.

Jeff shot a look of disbelief at his mother. "Momma, you promised!"

His mother smiled. "I know," she whispered. "But I'm so proud of you."

"So, Jeff," Mrs. Walker said, "the reason we wanted to have this meeting with you was to ensure that the community stays safe from the gangs. It's not just for our sake, but for yours, too — because this is your community as well as ours. So . . . we've written down a few things that maybe you could do." She pulled a list from her pocket and began to read. "When your mother finishes your uniform, we want you to wear it and patrol the neighborhood three times a week."

I don't believe this, Jeff thought.

From a corner of the room, the teenage boy took Jeff's picture.

"Next," said Mrs. Walker, "we would like to put another telephone in your apartment with call-waiting. We'll call it the Meteor Phone — just like Batman's phone on the TV show. And the Meteor Phone will be paid for by the community. We will only call in emergencies, or if someone hears or sees something."

Mr. Reed leaned over and whispered to Jeff, "That's fair."

"And, Jeff, we want you to tell the gangs, the junkies, the drug dealers, the pimps, and the prostitutes to get out of our community. And we would like to meet with you every Thursday from three-thirty to five-thirty, right here, to make special requests for things you can do. And finally . . . we would like you to fly some of the senior citizens to the hospital in emergencies. That's all."

The crowd applauded again.

"Now," Mrs. Walker said, "Here's something for you to dream about." She went to the wall behind her and pulled a cord. A banner rolled down. It read, METEOR MAN PATROLS HERE. GOLDEN LORDS BEWARE! The crowd jumped to its feet, giving Jeff a standing ovation.

The people around Jeff patted him on the back and shook his hand. Jeff nodded and smiled at them all. He thought, maybe if I have plastic surgery and change my name . . .

In the corner, the teenage boy looked at his photo in astonishment. It was a photo of a green blob wearing Jeff's clothes.

Later, Jeff talked it over with Ellington as they went for a walk.

"I *am not* scared," Jeff barked. "I just don't want to be a crime fighter. So I got superpowers? So what?"

"What a waste," Ellington answered.

Jeff barked. "What if I'm flying through the air, and suddenly I just fall from the sky?"

"What if you don't?" Ellington replied.

"I'm scared of heights, you know."

"Fly low."

"You've got an answer for everything, don't you? I don't want to talk about this anymore."

"That's what you always used to say to Stacy," Ellington barked.

"Now don't start getting on me about how I treated Stacy. You're no better than

I am. Stacy didn't like it when I said I wanted to date other women — but you do the same thing. You chase every female mutt on the street!"

"Yeah," Ellington barked. "I'm a *dog*!"

"This is going no place. Let's drop it."

"Whatever you say . . . *Chickenman*," Ellington barked.

"Don't call me chicken!" Jeff snarled. "I don't want to fight crime because that's what the police are for."

"The police need help."

"I can't just take the law into my own hands!"

About a second too late, Jeff noticed a young woman walking nearby. She was looking at him as if he'd lost his marbles. The woman was walking with her dog, and the dog started barking at Jeff, saying, "You sound like a chicken to me!"

"Nobody was talking to you, *mutt*!" Ellington barked.

The dog barked at Ellington, "Your momma!"

The two dogs lunged at each other. Jeff and the woman separated them.

"Sorry about that," Jeff told the woman, embarrassed.

"Don't worry," the woman said, walking away as quickly as she could.

The next morning, sitting alone in the school cafeteria, Jeff thought things over. The Meteor Man thing had really gotten out of hand. Fight the gangs? Patrol the neighborhood in some homemade Halloween costume? When the Golden Lords got finished laughing, they'd gang up and beat him to a pulp. The two M's on his costume would stand for something different then: Mince Meat.

And anyway, what about his free time? What about his music? He had his own life to lead. Nobody else seemed to be interested in that, though. No, it was just "Meteor Man this" and "Meteor Man that." And the Meteor Phone! Now that was the last straw. He'd never have any privacy again!

He poured cream in his coffee and opened his briefcase. *The Faceless Crusader* comic book, the one that had fallen out of Dre's pocket, was on top. Jeff blew on his coffee. When he looked down at it, it was frozen solid. His breath had turned it to ice!

Just then, Stacy walked up. "Good morning, Jeff. Uh . . . frozen coffee?"

"Well," Jeff said, "I, uh . . . I don't like ice cream much, but I love ice coffee." To convince her, he smiled and licked his cup of frozen coffee.

Stacy looked in his briefcase and saw the comic book. "You read *The Faceless Crusader*?" she said.

"Oh . . . one of my students . . ."

"I *love* the Faceless Crusader!" Stacy said. "You never even knew I collected comic books."

"That's not true." Jeff was lying through his teeth. "I remembered you collected comic books. And Ol' Faceless is one of the best. I love it."

"So you read this one?" Stacy said.

"Twice," Jeff said. "I couldn't put it down."

She took the comic book out of the briefcase and looked at it. "Well, if you read it, Jeff, why is the safety seal still unbroken? This hasn't even been opened yet. You didn't read this — you probably just took it from one of your students. You haven't changed a bit." She tossed the comic book back in Jeff's briefcase.

"I did read it!" Jeff said.

"You did not!"

"Did so!"

"All right, then," Stacy said. "If you read it, tell me what happens in the beginning."

"Well, um . . ." Jeff eased his fingers toward the comic book and touched it. A green spark flew from Jeff's hand unseen by Stacy. "Yes. The beginning. Do you mean before or after he's trapped in the plutonium crate by the evil doctor Michalfink?"

"You did read it!" Stacy said, smiling suddenly. She sat down next to Jeff. "I could talk about the Faceless Crusader for hours! Every time he's in the clutches of one of those evil villains, I love hearing him say, 'I will make a difference!' Then, poof! He fights and wins."

"Yeah . . . I love that, too," Jeff said.

"You know, Jeff . . . if only we could get that across to the kids. That *they* have power. That *they* can make a difference and do something positive. But it's so hard when TV and movies fill their heads with such garbage . . . and the only role models they see are drug dealers. I'm sorry — I'm talking too much. Your ice coffee is melting."

"No, no!" Jeff took a few licks from his

ice coffee, then said, "I agree with you completely. I look around at these inner city schools, and I see the smartest kids becoming drug dealers and gang members. It's such a waste! Kids say they hate math, and they know the difference between an eighth, a gram, and a kilo of some drug. Instead of being drug pushers, these kids could become scientists. They could discover the cure for cancer or AIDS. Just think . . . one of them could even be president one day."

"I know!" Stacy said, excited.

The bell rang.

"Well," Jeff said. "Time to get to class."

"Yeah. I'll see you later, Jeff. And . . . thanks for listening to me."

That evening, Jeff walked to his parents' house with Michael.

"Before we eat dinner," Jeff said, "I'm gonna lay it on the line with my parents. I'm gonna tell 'em I don't want to be *Meteor Man*."

"What about the neighbors? What are you gonna tell them?"

"The same thing," Jeff said, ringing his parents' doorbell.

When the door opened, forty people yelled, "SURPRISE!"

"What is this!" Jeff shouted. "It's not my birthday!"

"We know," his mother said. "But we had to do something to show how proud we are of our Meteor Man!"

"Everybody's excited about seeing your superpowers!" his father said.

The children in the living room began chanting, "Meteor Man! Meteor Man!"

Jeff's heart sank.

What he thought would be a quiet dinner turned into *The Meteor Man Show* — starring the very reluctant Jeff Reed. Everywhere he looked, there was someone wanting him to do some trick.

A child held up a deck of cards and said, "Jeff! What's the top card?"

Jeff rolled his eyes. He used his X-ray vision on the deck of cards and said, "Three of clubs."

"Right!"

A woman from down the street broke two eggs into a frying pan and said, "Can you cook 'em for me, Jeff?"

Jeff sighed. He made lasers come out of

his eyes and aimed them at the eggs. In a few seconds, they were fried.

Mr. Reed was standing behind a group of children. "Jeff, these kids want you to make them fly."

"Me first! Me first!" all the kids said at once.

Jeff pointed his finger at the first kid, and he floated up into the air. Then Jeff gently let him down. He did the same thing with all twelve kids in the room.

But the requests kept coming.

"Jeff, let's go outside so we can see you fly!"

"Jeff, let's go to the drugstore. You can use your X-ray vision and see what the winning lottery ticket is. I'll cut you in for half!"

"Jeff, talk to my French poodle. I want to see if he really speaks French!"

"Jeff, let's go to the racetrack tomorrow."

"Jeff!"

"Jeff!"

"Jeff!"

Every time his name was shouted, Jeff felt his blood pressure go up. Finally, he snapped. "ENOUGH! Would everybody just stop! I can't believe what's going on in here. You're turning my life into a circus act. I come over here for a quiet dinner with my parents and find out the main course is *me!*" He looked at his parents. "And, Momma and Daddy, I'm really disappointed in you. The show's over. Good night!"

Fuming, Jeff walked out of the apartment, down the stairs, and outside. Then he stopped cold. Just up the street, there was an ambulance and a TV crew. A woman was being carried into the ambulance on a stretcher. Jeff strained to see who it was, and then gasped.

It was Mrs. Walker.

Near the ambulance, a young woman reporter was interviewing Mr. Moses. "It's awful," he said, looking like he was about to cry. "I've known her . . . for twelve years."

The reporter turned to the camera and said, "Another senseless gang beating . . . where no one saw anything or heard anything. A sixty-one-year-old woman is badly hurt. I'm Janice Farrell reporting for Channel Three News."

Janice Farrell and the TV crew packed up and left. Jeff rushed down and hugged Mr. Moses. "I'm sorry."

"Jeff, I . . ." Mr. Moses began to cry. "I saw the whole thing."

"Poor Mrs. Walker," Jeff said. And then he had a terrible thought. Maybe she wouldn't have been beaten up . . . if he had been patrolling the neighborhood, like everyone wanted him to. Suddenly, Jeff felt very guilty.

But he felt something else, too: determined. He thought of what Stacy had said that morning — that kids needed to know they could make a difference. Well, maybe what they needed was an example. Maybe they needed to see someone else making a difference. I can be that someone, Jeff thought.

He would take on the gangs. They had beaten up a sixty-one-year-old woman — now they'd have somebody a little tougher to deal with.

It was time for Jeff to become . . . Meteor Man.

Chapter 9

Saturday. Early morning. The sunlight sparkled off the waters of the river. Along the bank, Michael and Ellington walked at a brisk pace. Beside them, dressed in gray sweats, flew Jeff Reed — a.k.a. Meteor Man.

"You can't fly any higher than that, huh?" Michael said.

"I told you, I'm afraid of heights. Four feet is as high as I want to go."

"Hope the Golden Lords never get any helicopters. If they do, you're gonna have a hard time catching them."

"How do you think I can fly *faster*?" Jeff said.

"Maybe . . . kick your feet. Like you're swimming."

Jeff tried it. He started to fly faster. But then he flipped over forward. He shot ahead of Michael and Ellington, flying upside down and calling "Michaaeelllll!"

Later in the day, Jeff strolled down his block carrying his briefcase. Then he heard screams coming from an alley. He stopped, looked both ways, then opened his briefcase. Inside was a gray sweatsuit with two M's on the chest, and a flowered sheet for a cape — his temporary costume. He changed into it with lightning speed, then ran quickly into the alley.

A man, who had his back to Jeff, was kicking a woman who lay on the ground. "Leave that woman alone!" Jeff shouted.

The man turned around. It was Mr. Moses.

On the ground, the woman, who was Michael in a wig, clicked a stopwatch. "Eight seconds . . . not bad! Now let's see how long it takes you to change back . . . go!"

With incredible speed, Jeff leapt back into his street clothes.

When he was done, Michael clicked the

watch. "Ten seconds. Pretty good. But, uh
. . . your fly is open."

Jeff looked disgusted, and snapped his
fingers.

Several times over the next few days,
Jeff dropped in on his mother to see how
she was coming with his costume. The first
time, she confidently handed him a bundle
of material, smiled, and said, "Go try this
on."

Jeff went alone into his parents' bedroom
and put on the costume. When he came out
into the living room, Mr. Reed and Michael
saw him — and howled with laughter.

Confused, Jeff went to look in the mirror.
Then he started laughing himself. The costume was red, black, and yellow, and had
shoulders that stretched out a foot on each
side.

"I thought you were Meteor Man," Mr.
Reed said, "not Shoulder Man!"

"Save me, Shoulder Man!" Michael
howled. "If you can fit through the door!"

"All right, that's enough," Jeff's mother
said. "Back to the drawing board."

* * *

Sitting in a hamburger joint, Michael pulled a folded-up sheet of paper from his pocket and said, "I've got it."

"Got what?" Jeff asked, his mouth full of french fries.

"Our ticket to success: the Meteor Man theme song. Check out these lyrics:

> *He's a brother who flies*
> *With muscular thighs*
> *Can smell criminals*
> *Like people who don't use Ban.*
> *Get ready for the Meteor Man."*

Jeff looked at Michael as if he were crazy, and ate more French fries.

COSTUME TRY-ON #2

Jeff walked into the living room wearing a costume that was yellow, pink, and powder blue — and had feathers on it. Feathers stuck out of the shoulders and ankles. A feather mask covered Jeff's face.

Michael began laughing so hard that at first he didn't make a sound. When he did, it was high-pitched and as loud as a siren.

Jeff's father looked at Jeff's mother. "Honey . . . is this a joke?" he asked.

"I like it," Michael said, and fell over sideways, laughing.

From behind his feather mask, Jeff glared at Michael.

Jeff's mother looked peeved. "Well, maybe if one of you comedians knew how to sew, you could make something better. All right . . . I'll try it again."

At lunch in the school cafeteria, Michael pulled out another sheet of folded paper, and said, "I worked some more on the Meteor Man theme song."

"Brother, here we go again," Jeff said.

Michael unfolded the paper and crooned:

He's flyin' low
But he ain't slow
Gangs don't have long —
'Cause this brother's strong!
Touches a book and knows what's in it,
His knowledge lasts for half a minute!
The Golden Lords saw him and ran —
They knew they couldn't beat Meteor Man!

"What do you think?" Michael asked. "Does it still need work?"

"That's a polite way of putting it," Jeff said.

Suddenly, Michael was looking behind Jeff. He said, "Well, look at who just walked in."

Jeff turned around. He saw Stacy. Walking next to her was a tall man as thin as a pencil. The cuffs of his pants were four inches above his shoes. He wore glasses so thick that his eyes were like fuzzy specks.

"Guess that's Stacy's new boyfriend," Michael said. "Hey, maybe if you put on that last Meteor Man costume, you two could have a nerd contest!"

"Stacy!" Jeff called out.

Stacy looked around and saw Jeff and Michael. Her expression seemed to say, *Guess I can't hide.* So she walked with her friend over to the table.

"Hi, guys," she said.

"Hi," Jeff said. "How are you?"

"Fine. Jeff, Michael, this is my friend Malik."

"My name used to be Chester," Malik said. "I just changed my name two weeks ago, and boy was my mom perturbed. But I told her to *chill*."

Jeff suddenly touched his eye. "Ow! I think my contact lens slipped. Stacy, could you check?"

Stacy sat down close to Jeff and looked in his eye. "Jeff, you don't wear contacts," she whispered.

"Where'd you find that guy . . . Disneyland?" Jeff whispered back.

"Be nice," Stacy hissed.

"I miss you," Jeff whispered.

Stacy looked at him a moment. "That's the first time you ever said that."

Just then, there was a booming sound — an explosion. Everyone in the cafeteria ran outside to see what had happened. Across the street, a car was on fire. Nearby, a woman was screaming, "Help! Help! My child's trapped inside!"

Jeff looked around him. Sure that no one was watching him, he drew a breath and blew a mighty gust of air toward the car. The flames went out. As the smoke billowed into the air, people rushed over to get the child out.

"Lucky thing that wind came along and

blew out the fire," Malik said. "But what was that funky *smell*?"

Uh-oh, Jeff thought. He remembered what he'd just eaten for lunch: liver and onions.

At night, in the park, Michael sat on a bench holding a boom box. Ellington sat at his feet. Jeff flew around in circles.

When he came to a stop, Michael told him, "I got the new theme song." He pushed a button on the boom box. Out came the sound of Michael's voice, singing:

The brother's strong
And I ain't wrong
He flies around
Close to the ground
Thieves beware, and don't be greedy or
You'll have to deal with our Man Me-te-or!

Jeff just looked at Michael. Then he looked at the boom box. With his eyes, he shot lasers at it and blew it to bits.

"Well, thanks a lot," Jeff said. He was talking to the telephone repairman, who had just installed a telephone jack in his living room.

"No problem," the repairman said.

Jeff opened the door for him to leave. When he did, Mrs. Harris and Mr. Moses were standing there. Mr. Moses had on still another of his toupees. This one looked like a dead raccoon.

Mrs. Harris was holding a shopping bag. She reached in and pulled out a telephone. It was a brilliant green, touch-tone phone with two bold M's at the center of the dial.

"Yeah!" Jeff yelled, excited. He ran over to plug it in.

Two seconds later, it rang.

Nervously, Jeff picked it up. "Hello . . . Meteor Man here."

Then he heard the voice of Mrs. Walker, who'd just come home from the hospital. "Just checking!"

COSTUME TRY-ON #3

From the living room, Jeff's mother called out, "Come on out, Jeff . . . we want to see how it looks!"

Jeff walked in. His father, his mother, and Michael were all sitting on the sofa.

96

When they saw him, their mouths fell open. For a while, no one spoke. Finally Mr. Reed said, "Jeff . . . you look . . . great."

"Way to go, Mrs. Reed!" Michael said.

Now, Jeff *looked* like a superhero. Form-fitting, gray body suit with green trunks — green suede boots with silver trim — green leather gloves — wide silver belt — long green cape — and two shining green letters in the center of his chest: MM.

"Look out!" Jeff shouted. "Look out, all you drug-dealing, hubcap-stealing, gun-shooting, store-looting, purse-grabbing, back-stabbing pimps, wimps, slugs, and thugs! *Meteor Man is born!*"

Chapter 10

Nighttime. Southeast Washington. Dark, littered, dangerous streets where even the police feared to go. Meteor Man flew through these streets . . . four feet off the ground.

He sailed past parked cars and looked into the distance. With his amazing night vision, he saw a crime in progress three blocks away: A young punk was snatching an old woman's purse.

Stretching out his arms and legs, putting his hands together and his feet together, Meteor Man went into *meteor speed*. He shot down the middle of the street like a man-sized bullet. He caught up to the running teenager and cruised alongside him.

"Excuse me, homeboy," Meteor Man said politely. "But I don't believe that purse belongs to you."

The teenager looked around. When he saw Meteor Man, he was so scared he dropped the purse. He kept running, his eyes still on Meteor Man, until he ran into a telephone pole and knocked himself out.

Jeff reached down for the purse and flew it back to the old woman.

"Thank you," she said, staring at his costume. "Are you the M & M Man?"

"No, ma'am. I'm Meteor Man. Have a nice evening."

The next night. The Community Day Care Center.

"All right! All right! Let's call this meeting to order!" Mr. Reed shouted. Finally, everyone stopped talking. "Now . . . can we hear, *one at a time*, ideas for what Meteor Man can do around the neighborhood? Now, who's first? One person at a time, please."

Everyone started yelling at once again.

"Meteor Man, my boyfriend said I was evil. Will you go over to his house and knock some sense into him?"

"Meteor Man, our dryer broke down. Could you come over and blow on our clothes?"

"Meteor Man, my daughter thinks you're cute. Here's her telephone number. Call after eight — that's when she gets home from Weight Watchers."

"Meteor Man — "

Jeff ran for the front door. His father called out, "Meteor Man! Where are you going?"

"Back out to patrol the streets. It's safer out there!"

Flying down the street, Meteor Man saw two thieves coming down a fire escape with a TV. Meteor Man flew over, grabbed onto the bottom of the fire escape, and climbed up.

One of the thieves looked down and said, "Who are you?"

"Who are *you*?" Meteor Man replied.

The thief pulled out a pistol. "We're TV repairmen."

"Oh," Meteor Man said, stroking his

chin. He reached for the TV's plug and touched it with his finger. Suddenly, the TV came on. The thieves stared in disbelief at *I Love Lucy*.

The thief said, "What the . . ."

Meteor Man pointed his finger at the TV. The volume went all the way up. Soon, the people inside the building were yelling.

"Hey, turn that down!"

"It's coming from outside!"

"Hey, that's somebody on the fire escape!"

"Call the cops!"

Meteor Man flew off, bullet-style, down the street. In the distance, but getting closer, was the sound of police sirens.

Flying along, Meteor Man — Jeff — thought about Stacy. Wish she could see me now, he thought. Then she'd be impressed. But he couldn't tell her the secret. Not yet.

In a tiny room, on the third floor of a dilapidated house, twelve people moved like zombies around a table, mixing and preparing drugs.

Suddenly the door fell in. In the doorway

stood Meteor Man. He took a deep breath and sent a strong wind into the room, blowing all the drugs into the air. Not a speck was left on the table — there was just one big drug-cloud hovering right below the ceiling.

Meteor Man disappeared down the stairs. The drug makers were left there, breathing in the drug-filled air.

Eleven-thirty P.M. A street lined with brownstones and small apartment buildings. On both sides of the street there were flashes of light, like matches being struck. But they weren't matches — they were gunshots. Two gangs, the Crips and the Bloods, were shooting at the police from behind parked cars.

Out of nowhere, Meteor Man landed in the middle of the street. Bullets bounced off his arms and shoulders. The sound of gunfire died away as the Crips and the Bloods and the policemen stopped shooting and just stared.

From behind a car, the leader of the Bloods shouted, "Who is *this*?"

On the other side of the street, the leader

of the Crips shouted, "Where'd he *come* from?"

Meteor Man shouted, "I want to talk. It's time to make peace. Put down your weapons and let's talk."

"It's a trick!" said the Blood leader.

"He's with the po-lice!" said the Crips leader.

They opened fire on Meteor Man. He was hit with bullets from every kind of handgun — from a .22-caliber pistol to a .44 magnum. Bullets ricocheted off of every part of his body.

Then the shooting stopped. Both sides had run out of bullets — except for one member of the Crips. He ran into the street with a sawed-off shotgun. At point-blank range, he fired into Meteor Man's stomach. When the smoke cleared, Meteor Man was yawning. He looked at the Crip and said, "Was there something you wanted?"

The Crip ran back behind the car.

"Now," Meteor Man said, "let's try that again. May I please talk to both sides."

Slowly, hesitantly, the leaders of each gang walked to the middle of the street. They stood on either side of Meteor Man, looking at him, and each other, with distrust.

Meteor Man looked from one of them to the other and said, "So what's the problem?"

The drughouse. Simon Hawkins, Uzi, and Goldilocks walked in, stepping over the door that had been kicked in by Meteor Man. They looked around them, unable to believe their eyes. On the other side of the room were the drug preparers, looking like people in a trance, white powder on their faces. They weren't doing a thing — just standing and staring.

Furious, Simon walked up and hollered, "What happened in here?"

One of the drug-preparers said, "A man in a cape . . . kicked the door in and . . . um . . . let's see."

Simon grabbed him by the collar. "You're high!"

"I didn't want to be. But he blew it in our faces! Then . . . what happened then? I forgot." Simon threw him to the floor, where he lay like a mat.

Simon's wireless telephone rang. He reached down, detached the phone from his belt, and said, "Hello? Yes, Mr. Byers, I'm here now. Oh . . . yes . . . of course. I'll take the first plane out in the morning. Good-bye."

He put the phone back on his belt. Turning to Uzi and Goldilocks, he said, "I've got to fly down to meet with Byers tomorrow. Something big's going down. While I'm gone, see what you can find out about this dude in the cape."

Chapter 11

Jeff stood in the bathroom, washing his gray tights in the sink. Michael sat in the living room watching the news with Ellington.

On TV, the reporter Janice Farrell was saying, "Congress has vetoed more spending for the public school system."

"Janice Farrell is so beautiful," Michael said. "If I met her one time, she would be my woman."

"Just like Whitney and Paula would be your women," Jeff said.

"Just wait till they meet me," Michael replied.

On TV, Janice Farrell said, ". . . And

there has been yet another sighting of the African-American male in a cape, fighting crime."

Michael lurched forward. "Jeff get in here! Quick!" Jeff rushed in.

"He has reportedly shut down fifteen drug houses, stopped eleven attempted robberies, and brought peace between two inner-city street gangs, the Bloods and the Crips, and the police," Janice Farrell continued. "The gangs have now vowed to work together to rebuild the communities they destroyed."

Jeff and Michael slapped five.

"So what are the Bloods and Crips really like?" Michael asked.

"Man, they are so cool. Snake, the leader of the Crips, and Poison, the leader of the Bloods, gave me their home phone numbers. I'm having them over for dinner."

"Yeah . . . whatever night it is, I'm busy," Michael said.

Janice Farrell continued. "Hollywood has jumped on the bandwagon, already making this episode into a movie. Denzel Washington has signed on to play the leader of the Bloods, and Wesley Snipes has agreed to play the leader of the Crips.

Spike Lee will direct, and Byron Allen will play the caped man."

Jeff and Michael frowned at each other, and said at the same time, "Byron Allen?"

Janice Farrell said, "Up next . . . an interview with the caped man!"

Jeff thought, I did an interview?

Michael said, "You did an interview?"

"No!"

They both watched the screen. Janice Farrell returned. Seated next to her was a man with a green pin-striped suit, more rings than a jewelry store, a cape made of burlap, and no front teeth.

"That's not me!" Jeff shouted.

"Yeah," Michael said. "You don't own a pinstripe."

Janice Farrell said, "Here with us, live, is the Caped Man. Welcome, Clarence James Carter the Third!"

"Thank you, Janice," said Clarence.

"People said they saw you fly away. Explain that."

"Well," Clarence said, chuckling, "I move so fast that people think I'm flying. I used to box . . . fast hands."

Michael and Jeff stared with open mouths.

"You have a police record for attempted burglary, auto theft . . ." Janice Farrell said.

Clarence smiled and said, "That's all behind me now, Janice. I'm a crime fighter now, and I just want to say to the criminals, BEWARE!"

Unable to take any more, Jeff turned off the TV. "That guy's got his share of nerve and somebody else's, too. I've got to straighten this out!"

Just then, there was a knock at the door. Jeff opened it, and his heart skipped a beat. Stacy was standing there.

"Hi," she said, smiling.

"Hi," Jeff said. "What are you . . . I mean . . ."

"I've been thinking a lot about you lately, Jeff," Stacy said. "And maybe I've been wrong. We've been through a lot together. And I do still have feelings for you."

Jeff thought he was dreaming. He hoped he wasn't — he had prayed for something like this to happen. "Oh, Stacy . . . these last four months have been crazy without you."

"They've been bad for me, too. Can I come in?"

"Of cour — " Jeff remembered something: the gray tights in the bathroom! Then he had a thought. He barked to Ellington, "Hide my uniform!" Then he turned back to Stacy, who was looking at him strangely now. "I got a cold," he told her.

Ellington raced to the bathroom and hid the boots, belt, and cape in the clothes hamper. Then he jumped, and jumped again, but couldn't reach the tights hanging from the shower curtain rod.

Michael walked over, trying to block Stacy's view of the bathroom. "Hi, Stacy," he said, smiling like a moron.

"Hi, Michael," she said. "Jeff, I'm not going to stay long. I just wanted to say I'm sorry for the way I've been acting, and I . . ." She paused, and her expression changed. Then she said, "Well, I guess you haven't missed me *too* much."

"What do you mean?"

"Who do those tights in your bathroom belong to?"

Jeff didn't know what to say, so he didn't say anything.

"They're mine," Michael said.

"*Yours?*" Stacy asked.

"Yeah . . . you know, sometimes pants aren't enough. My legs get so cold, so I always wear a pair of stockings or panty hose underneath. For warmth. Doesn't everyone?"

"You're lying," Stacy said. "And Jeff . . . you haven't changed." She looked like she was about to cry. "Good-bye!"

"Stacy, you're wrong! I — " Jeff said.

She left and slammed the door.

Meanwhile . . .

In a large, plush office in South America, twenty-five well-dressed people sat around a long, long table. The people had come from many different countries — they were the world's biggest drug suppliers. Among them was Simon Hawkins.

At the head of the table stood Alexander Byers. He had a tailor-made suit, manicured hands, white hair, and a fierce expression on his face. He held up a newspaper for all to see. The headline read, FLYING MAN DESTROYS BILLION-DOLLAR DRUG SHIPMENT HIDDEN IN TRUCK. The photo showed Meteor Man lifting the truck and dumping the drugs onto a trash heap.

Byers growled, "What is this? Is this a *joke*? If it is, I'm not laughing."

The table was silent. Finally, one man cleared his throat and said, "My sources tell me it's an African-American male who's freaking out on drugs."

Byers ignored him and looked at Simon. "What do you know about this?"

"Nothing, Mr. Byers," Simon said.

"This started in your territory."

"But I don't know anything, Mr. Byers," Simon said. He was thinking, *It must be that dude Uzi and Goldilocks saw fly up the pole.* But he couldn't let Byers know that he knew who it was. Byers would want to know why Simon hadn't stopped him yet.

Byers told the group, "They say this guy can fly. Well, I don't want him to fly anymore. Gentlemen, I'm putting a price on his head. One million dollars alive . . . two million *dead.*"

Between two condemned buildings in southeast Washington, there was a vacant lot. No grass grew in the lot. There was just dirt and some trash — scraps of paper, broken bottles, and rusted, abandoned cars.

Meteor Man walked around the lot. He cleared away all the garbage, shoving it to the edge of the lot. Next, he ripped the fender from one of the old rusted cars and used it to plow the dirt. Then he grabbed two huge sacks filled with seeds. With lightning speed, he flew around the lot, pouring seeds into the ground. When the seeds were planted, he touched the ground with his hands. The whole lot glowed green.

Meteor Man looked at the sky. Some clouds were passing overhead. He drew a breath and sent a powerful shaft of arctic air into the sky, freezing one of the clouds. The cloud began to rain on the dirt and seeds. Smiling, Meteor Man flew away.

Nighttime. In a parking lot, walking through rows of cars, was Clarence James Carter the Third. But now, instead of wearing a burlap cape and talking with reporter Janice Farrell, he was wearing a sweatshirt — and about to steal a car.

He stopped in front of a Mercedes Benz. Humming a Temptations song, he picked the door lock, hot-wired the ignition, and drove off. Cruising down the street, he smiled and sang.

Then he heard another voice singing along with him.

Clarence looked around to see where the voice was coming from. Then a terrified look crossed his face. Flying beside the car, singing "My Girl," was Meteor Man!

"Who are *you*?" Clarence shouted.

"I'm Meteor Man! I'm the crime fighter you pretended to be on TV, you toothless fake!"

Reaching down, Meteor Man lifted up the car — and flew with it up into the air.

"Please, Meteor Man! I'm sorry — I won't do it anymore! Please put me down!"

Meteor Man looked down. The cars on the street below looked like little bugs. "Wait a minute," he said to himself. "I'm more than four feet off the ground. I'm more than four *hundred* feet off the ground. And I'm not afraid! This is fun!" He shouted to Clarence, "I'll put you down . . . if you promise to tell everybody the truth!"

"Okay — okay! I'll tell them, Meteor Man!"

* * *

At home, Jeff watched TV in his living room with Michael and Ellington.

On the TV screen, a long line of homeless people stood in line near a garden. They were all smiling. One by one, the homeless people walked up and were handed fruits and vegetables. The apples, pears, carrots, potatoes, and beans were the largest anyone had ever seen. There were tomatoes as big as basketballs and cornstalks six feet high; there were monstrous heads of lettuce, and a vine with grapes the size of baseballs.

Janice Farrell appeared on screen and said, "This is a miracle! The garden in the middle of the ghetto. It will feed thousands and thousands. Who's behind this? We reported a few nights ago that the caped man was Clarence James Carter the Third, but the Bloods and Crips say that it isn't Mr. Carter. The caped hero likes to be called *Meteor Man*! No one knows his real identity."

Jeff and Michael did a high-five.

"Well, whoever you are," Janice Farrell said, "keep up the good work. And Meteor Man, if you're ever in my neighborhood, lunch is on me. I'm Janice Farrell with Channel Three News."

"All right!" Jeff shouted. "Now they know the truth!"

The next day, Jeff walked into the crowded cafeteria and looked around. Then he spotted Stacy. He walked over and sat down beside her.

"Can I talk to you for a second?" he whispered. "I want to explain about . . . the tights in my bathroom."

"Jeff, you don't have to explain anything to me," Stacy whispered. "I shouldn't have come by. I felt like such a fool. It just reminded me of how our relationship was. You never appreciated me."

"Why do you say I didn't appreciate you?"

"You never showed it, that's for sure. You never brought me flowers, or candy . . ."

"I never did that because any fool can buy flowers and candy!" Jeff hissed.

At that moment, Malik walked up to the table. In one hand he held a bouquet of roses, and in the other he had a box of chocolates. "Surprise!" he said to Stacy, grinning. "I knew it was your lunch break. I just brought these to show you I was thinking about you. Oh, uh, hi, Jeff."

Stacy accepted the roses and chocolates with a broad grin.

Jeff wanted to throw up.

At the end of the day, Jeff sat alone in his classroom. The students had left, and Jeff was preparing to leave himself.

Then Goldilocks walked into the room, followed by Uzi. After them came six Baby Lords. Finally, in walked Simon Hawkins. He had his long black coat draped over his shoulders, and he carried a Slinky. While Goldilocks, Uzi, and the Baby Lords stood like soldiers, Simon walked slowly over to Jeff's desk. He sat down on the edge of it and played with the Slinky.

"Slinkys move like life," he said, with a mysterious smile. "You never know how a Slinky will move . . . just like life. In one second, everything can change — for better or for worse."

Simon put the Slinky down. He leaned closer to Jeff, and said, "Isn't that right . . . Meteor Man?"

Chapter 12

"Tell me, Meteor Man," Simon said to Jeff. "What's your secret?"

Jeff tried to decide what to do to Simon first. Should he singe him with his laser eyes . . . should he take a deep breath and blow him back out the door . . . or should he just give him an old-fashioned punch in the face? But then Jeff remembered — he couldn't reveal his identity. "I'm sorry," he said to Simon. "You must have me confused with someone else. What did you call me — *Meter Maid*?"

"You're Meteor Man," Simon said. "We both know it. Why don't you join me? I'll make it worth your while."

Just then, Michael walked into the room. He said to Jeff, "Excuse me, Mr. Reed, I hate to interrupt, but you're going to be late for that meeting with the principal."

"Oh, yes," said Jeff. "Thanks for reminding me."

"And did you hear the latest about Meteor Man?" Michael asked. "He just destroyed another drug house! Isn't that great?" he said, looking at Simon.

"That's wonderful," Simon said sarcastically. Simon thought, Maybe this isn't the guy. I'll have to watch him some more.

"I'm sorry," Simon said to Jeff. "I must have been mistaken."

"No problem," Jeff told him.

Simon, Uzi, Goldilocks, and the Baby Lords left the room. When they were gone, Jeff said to Michael, "Thanks, old buddy. That was a close one."

"No problem," Michael said. "I saw them come in."

"Let's get out of here," Jeff said.

That night, while Jeff and Ellington slept, a man came into the apartment through the living room window. The man walked quietly into the bathroom and

119

searched through a pile of clothes. Finally, he found the Meteor Man uniform. He took it and went back out the window. . . .

The next morning was Saturday. Jeff got up and stumbled into the kitchen for some cereal. He turned on the radio and listened while he ate.

Suddenly, Ellington came running in. He barked, "Jeff! Your uniform is gone!"

"Are you sure?!" Jeff barked.

"Yes!"

Jeff began looking around frantically. "It's gotta be here somewhere," he muttered. "Or else . . . the Golden Lords must have taken it!"

While he was still looking, he heard the DJ on the radio say, "I'm coming at you live from the Union Hills Mall this Saturday morning. I've got T-shirts and cassettes to give away, but first . . . we have a surprise visitor. The man who's been cleaning up this city . . . Meteor Man!"

Jeff froze.

"Good morning, Meteor Man, and thanks for stopping by."

"Well, thank you," said a second voice on the radio. "I'm just trying to make D.C.

safe again, especially for all the beautiful, sexy ladies here. And . . . I've brought along a cassette of my theme song."

"That's Michael!" Jeff shouted.

Jeff got dressed in a flash and bolted out to his car. He drove toward Union Hills Mall muttering, "What does that nut think he's doing?"

Meanwhile, another car was headed toward the mall. In this car were Uzi, Goldilocks, and Simon Hawkins. They had the car radio on. Michael's voice came out of it, saying, "And I would like to invite my favorite TV anchor, Janice Farrell, to join me for a meal."

"Your last meal," Uzi said.

He, Goldilocks, and Simon pulled out their pistols and screwed on silencers. Simon laughed and said, "What's two million dollars split three ways?"

Minutes later, Jeff's car screeched to a stop at the back of the mall. Jeff leapt out, ran to a door, and pulled the handle. It was locked. He ripped the door off its hinges and ran inside.

Inside the mall, Simon, Uzi, and Goldilocks walked quickly through the shoppers. They were headed toward the other end of the mall — to the radio broadcast booth.

In the booth sat Michael, wearing the Meteor Man suit — plus a black mask. He was talking to a young woman in a short dress. "My identity must remain a secret," he was saying to her. "But if you give me your telephone number . . ."

One floor up, Jeff moved quickly through the crowd, his eyes searching for Michael. But then, glancing down at the level below, he saw the Golden Lords. He raced for the stairs.

"There he is," Uzi said, pointing to Michael, a hundred feet away.

Michael glanced up and saw the Golden Lords headed for him. "I gotta go, baby," he said to the woman in the short dress.

"Are you gonna fly away?" she asked him.

"Nah, I don't wanna show off."

Michael started running away from the Golden Lords.

The Lords pulled their guns from their jackets.

Jeff made it to the bottom of the stairs. With his eyes, he shot a laser at Uzi's pistol, destroying the hammer. Uzi tried to fire, but couldn't. Jeff shot another laser at Goldilocks's pistol. The laser made the gun so hot that Goldilocks dropped it. Jeff was aiming a third laser at Simon's pistol — but then a heavyset woman moved right in front of Simon, blocking Jeff's view.

Ten feet behind Michael, Simon raised his pistol.

Jeff aimed a very thin laser — at the heavyset woman's backside. She began to scream, flailing her arms wildly, in every direction. With one of her swipes she hit Simon, and his gun flew out of his hand.

Next, Jeff pointed his finger at Michael, causing Michael to float up to the ceiling. The crowd began to applaud and whistle. Still pointing at Michael, Jeff began to jog toward the exit — and Michael began moving through the air, looking like he was Meteor Man flying.

Picking up his pistol from the floor, Simon noticed Jeff pointing up and running. Then he looked up at Michael, flying awkwardly. "Ah-ha," Simon said to himself.

When Jeff and Michael were outside, Michael said, "I'm sorry, man. I was going to ask you if I could borrow the uniform. I just wanted the DJ to play your theme song. And I thought I could meet Janice Farrell!"

"Michael, you've done some dumb things before, but this tops them all! You could have been killed! Now, take off that uniform."

"Jeff, let me explain — "

Jeff pointed at Michael again, and Michael floated once more into the air. But this time, he began twirling around — so fast that the boots, gloves, cape, and tights flew off. When he was down to his underwear, Jeff let him fall to the ground. Jeff picked up his uniform and got in the car.

"Jeff, I'm sorry!" Michael said. "Don't leave me here in my underwear!"

Jeff drove away.

That evening, the Community Day Care Center looked like a ballroom. There was music playing and people were dancing. Balloons and streamers hung from the walls. Then the music died down, and people began singing, "For he's a jolly good fellow, for he's a jolly good fellow . . ." Several people wheeled a giant cake across the floor. The writing on the cake said, "Thank you, Meteor Man!"

They wheeled the cake up to Jeff. Jeff, dressed as Meteor Man, smiled and said, "You all didn't have to do this."

"Jeff — uh — Meteor Man, this comes from the bottom of our hearts," Mrs. Walker said. "We want to say thank you for making our community safe again."

The crowd applauded and whistled.

"And now that *our* community is safe," Mrs. Walker continued, "we want to talk to you about expanding. We ALL have family in different cities that need your help, and . . ."

Just then came the sound of gunshots from outside. Everyone stopped talking. They all looked helplessly at Jeff.

Jeff ran out the door, with the whole crowd behind him. Outside, Jeff's mother lay in the middle of the street, surrounded by a crowd of bystanders.

"Momma!"

Jeff ran toward her, the crowd on his heels. His mother, who was unharmed, looked up at Jeff and shook her head no. The next second, the bystanders turned around.

"Surprise!" Simon Hawkins yelled. It was the Golden Lords, all holding guns.

Uzi picked Jeff's mother up off the ground and shoved her into Jeff's arms.

Simon yelled, "We just came by to give you a message!"

And the Golden Lords pointed their guns at the crowd.

Chapter 13

"No!" Jeff shouted.

The Golden Lords opened fire on Jeff's neighbors. Screams and bullets filled the air.

But Jeff, moving at blinding speed, flew back and forth, catching the bullets in his hands. He caught one as it was about to hit Mr. Moses' chest; he caught another as it was about to go into his father's head. But the people in the crowd ran farther away from each other, and the bullets started flying farther apart. Jeff thought, Oh no! If there's a bullet I don't catch —

But suddenly, Simon raised his arm, and the shooting stopped. "Like I said," he shouted, "we just wanted to bring you a message, Meteor Man. It's this: You can't be everywhere at once and save everybody. So long . . . I gotta buy some more bullets!"

Right on cue, a BMW came to a stop beside the Golden Lords. They jumped in, and the car screeched away.

Jeff watched the BMW disappear down the street. Then he looked at his hands, which were still holding the bullets. He let the bullets fall to the ground. And then he noticed something. . . .

His hand was bleeding.

The next morning, Jeff sat in his kitchen, drinking a cup of coffee and thinking. He wondered if maybe he was doing the community more harm than good. He had tried to protect the people around him; but because of him, those people might be in more danger now than ever before. The Golden Lords didn't care who they had to hurt to maintain their reign of terror. And they were right . . . Meteor Man couldn't protect everybody.

Especially since his powers seemed to be disappearing.

Some of the bullets had actually pierced the skin of his hand, which meant he wasn't as tough as before. Come to think of it, he had been feeling a little weaker the last couple of days. Jeff tried using his X-ray vision on his kitchen wall. He couldn't see all the way through it; he could just see a couple of inches inside it. This was depressing.

What should he do? The people in the community needed someone to protect them. On the other hand, the harder Jeff fought against the Golden Lords, the harder they would strike back against the community. Not to mention . . . the weaker Jeff got, the better his chances of getting killed himself.

Jeff barked to Ellington, "Hey, Ellington! Come here! I need to talk to you!"

Ellington came running in. "I need to talk to you," Jeff barked. "What do you think I should do? Should I keep on being Meteor Man, even though I'm getting weaker?"

Ellington began barking back.

"What's that?" Jeff barked. "I couldn't understand you."

Ellington barked some more. Jeff

strained to hear, but all his ear could pick up were pieces of words. He was losing his ability to understand Ellington, too.

"Oh, *noooooo*," Jeff said, putting his face in his hands.

Just then, he heard a voice from outside. "Jeff, Jeff, help!" It was Mrs. Harris. "Come before she gets hurt!"

Oh, no, Jeff thought, who are the Golden Lords threatening now? Still in his pajamas, Jeff ran to the window and flew out. He saw Mrs. Harris standing on the sidewalk, but no one else. Jeff flew down to her. He tried to land on his feet right beside her, but he missed — and fell with a loud crash into some trash cans.

"I'm here," Jeff shouted, picking himself up. "What's wrong?"

Mrs. Harris looked horrified. "It's Jenny! She's stuck on the ledge!"

Jeff looked at Mrs. Harris. He didn't know whether to scream at her or laugh at her. "Your *cat*? You got me out here in my pajamas because your cat is stuck on the ledge?"

Mrs. Harris looked offended. "Well, she's human, too."

"No she's not, she's — ah, never mind. Wait a minute."

Jeff jumped off the ground, but couldn't fly. He jumped again; he went higher this time, but still didn't take off. Finally, he backed up, took a running start, and jumped — and this time he flew, just long enough to grab Jenny. Then he lost control. Still holding Jenny, he fell onto the hood of a car. Jenny ran back to Mrs. Harris.

Jeff followed, in slight pain. He said, "This is the last time I do something like this! What if I hadn't been around?"

"Jeff, why'd you have so much trouble flying?" Mrs. Harris asked. "What's wrong?"

"Nothing's wrong . . . it's early in the morning. I'm still sleepy, that's all."

Then, from the corner of his eye, Jeff saw Dre and Squirrel. They were sitting on bikes, on the other side of the street. They had been watching him the whole time. When they saw Jeff looking, they rode away.

"Hey!" Jeff yelled. He took off running after them. Just as they were about to round a corner on their bikes, Jeff grabbed them by their shoulders.

"Let us go!" Squirrel hollered.

"And where you going? Huh?" Jeff asked. "Going to tell your friends the Golden Lords what you just saw?"

"What if we are?" Dre said.

"Why do you want to hang around with those guys for? You wanna be cool, is that it? Yeah — you're gonna look real cool in a year or two when you're lying in an alley somewhere with a gunshot wound!"

"So what?" Dre said. "What you care? Let us go!"

"I do care!" Jeff shouted. "You think I'd be out here in *pajamas* yelling at you two if I didn't care?"

"You don't care about me!" Dre said. "If you did, why'd you call my mother instead of telling them boys not to make fun of me?"

Jeff sighed. "Dre . . . sometimes teachers don't do all they should. Because we're human, too. But you gotta give us a chance. Do you really think the Golden Lords care more about you than I do?"

"Maybe they don't," Squirrel said. "But if we don't get back to them now they'll hurt us. Let us go, please."

Jeff let them go. They rode away, out of sight.

The next morning, as Jeff was walking up the steps to the school, he heard a voice behind him. "Jeff!" He stopped and turned around. It was Michael.

"Can I talk to you for a minute?"

"Sure," Jeff said.

They walked inside to Jeff's empty classroom. "You don't have to speak to me," Michael said. "I just want to say I'm sorry I acted so stupid the other day. I had no right to take your uniform. Can you forgive me?"

Jeff smiled. "Sure, I forgive you . . . Meteor Man." They shook hands. Then Jeff drew his hand back; it was still sore from the bullets.

"You're losing your powers, aren't you?" Michael asked sadly.

Jeff nodded his head.

"I figured out something," Michael said. "When the meteor hit you, it filled your body with particles that gave you that power. But most of those particles have dissolved now. That's why you're . . . getting weaker."

"So that's what it is," Jeff said. "Of course, understanding it doesn't make it any easier to take."

"Well, look at it this way, Jeff. Just for a while, you were able to do what no one ever did before. That's something, isn't it?"

"Yeah, it's something . . . but it's not enough. Not for this community. Oh, man, I'm feeling weak. Tired. I'm gonna go home early today."

Jeff did go home early. On the way, he felt so tired he could hardly walk. He went into his building and just about crawled up the steps. Once inside the apartment, he stumbled to his bedroom and collapsed face-down on the bed. In two seconds, he was in a deep, deep sleep.

A few minutes later, from outside, there came a deafening roar. It drowned out every other sound in the neighborhood. It sounded like an earthquake — but louder.

Jeff slept through it.

On the street, Mrs. Walker, who was sweeping, looked around to see where the sound was coming from. She stepped into the street and glanced to the right, then to the left. Then her mouth fell open. "Oh, no."

Three Golden Lords came thundering down the street on motorcycles. They came to a stop a few feet away from Jeff's building.

Mrs. Walker dropped her broom and ran up the steps. "Jeff! Jeff!" Mrs. Walker screamed. The Golden Lords followed close behind her.

Inside, Ellington stood on his hind legs, watching the scene from the window. When he saw the Lords coming into the building, he ran to Jeff's bedside and barked as loudly as he could. But Jeff wouldn't wake up. The Meteor Phone began ringing off the hook. Jeff snored through it all.

Mrs. Walker reached Jeff's apartment and pounded on the front door. "Jeff! Jeff!"

She looked behind her, expecting to see the Golden Lords coming. Instead, she saw three figures emerge from the shadows: Alexander Byers and two hitmen. "Thanks," Byers told Mrs. Walker. "We didn't know which apartment it was."

Inside, Ellington grabbed Jeff's collar in his mouth and dragged him off the bed. He hit the floor with a thud. Using all his strength, Ellington dragged Jeff around to the other side of the bed. Then he knocked over the clothes hamper and began piling clothes on top of Jeff, hiding his body. Finally, Ellington ran to the living room windows, jumped up, and hit the latch. The windows flew open.

In the hall, Byers pushed Mrs. Walker out of the way and one of the hit men began kicking the door. On the fifth kick, his foot went all the way through the wood. Using his shoulder, he knocked a gaping hole in the middle of the door and stepped inside. Byers and the second hit man followed.

Guns drawn, the hit men ran into the bedroom. They looked around, but didn't see anyone.

In the living room, Byers stood in front of the open windows. "He got away," Byers muttered to himself.

Then, Simon, Uzi, and Goldilocks came into the apartment. When Simon saw Byers, a frightened look appeared on his face. "Mr. Byers, what are you doing here?" he said.

"I'm doing your job," Byers said.

"I have it under control," Simon told him.

"You let him get away twice."

"He's losing his powers," Simon said. "I got him. I'll finish him off, and my territory will be back to normal."

"It better be," Byers growled. "Or maybe you'll be losing your powers, too!" Byers and the hitmen stormed out of the apartment.

Simon looked furious. "This Meteor Man character has gotten me into too much hot water. We've got to finish him off fast. In the meantime . . . get the other Lords over here. We should leave our friend a little calling card."

Goldilocks picked up the phone and called the other Lords. Then the three of them went down to the street and waited. A few minutes later, twenty more Lords roared onto the scene on motorcycles.

"You know what to do," Simon told them.

The Lords spread out. They began dumping garbage in the street and smashing car windshields.

From their windows, Mrs. Harris, Mrs. Walker, and Mr. Moses watched in horror.

Chapter 14

Hours later, Jeff woke up. When he opened his eyes, his mother was sitting on the side of his bed. His father and Michael were standing nearby.

"Whoa," Jeff said. "What happened?"

"The Golden Lords paid the neighborhood a little visit," his father replied.

"Why didn't somebody come get me?"

"We tried . . ." Michael said. "But you wouldn't wake up. I think I figured it out. The meteor that hit you changed your molecular structure — giving you powers. But when you use the powers, it takes a lot out of you. So while your body reenergizes, you sleep. That's why you slept so hard today."

Jeff thought about this, then said, "Does that mean . . . I now have my superpowers back?"

"No," Michael said, sadly. "That means you've now regained the strength of a normal human."

Jeff's head fell back on the pillow. "Great," he said. "It'll take more than a normal human to stop the Golden Lords."

"We've been talking about that, Jeff," his mother said. "Maybe you should leave town."

"Momma, I can't run away. I can't just desert the community."

"Nobody's saying you should run away," Michael said. "But you can't fight the whole gang, especially now. Just leave town for a few weeks."

"I can't. This is my home."

Later, there was a meeting at the Community Day Care Center. Walking there with Michael, Jeff gazed around at the neighborhood, which now looked like a combat zone. Trash and broken glass were everywhere. Two men nailed plywood over what had been a store window. Two policemen were questioning a neighbor. The neighbor just kept shaking his head.

Jeff and Michael walked into the Center. The meeting was already in progress; so many people were talking that no one saw them come in.

Mrs. Harris was saying, "What are we supposed to do? Wait like sitting ducks for the gang to come back?"

"It was never this bad before," Mr. Moses said. "They've started a war on this community, and we can't win it."

"We wouldn't be in this situation if it weren't for Jeff Reed!" a woman said. "If we could get him out of the neighborhood, we could make a deal with the gang."

"Let's vote on it," Mr. Moses said.

Jeff felt as if he'd been stabbed in the back. "You don't have to vote . . . I'll leave," he told them.

Everyone turned around and saw him. Mrs. Walker and Mr. Moses looked ashamed.

"I'm sorry about what happened tonight," Jeff said. "But I feel even sorrier watching what's going on in this room.

140

Can't you *see*? The gang isn't that power-ful — it's just that everybody's afraid to stand up to them. How can we stop the gangs and the crime if we act like we don't see them? Everybody complains about how the police don't do enough. But what right do we have to complain when we don't do *anything*? Man . . . I may not have X-ray vision anymore, but now I can *really* see what's going on."

Jeff looked at the crowd; most of them were looking at the floor, and none of them said a word. Jeff opened his mouth to say more, then closed it again, and walked out.

He went home and started packing. He threw his suitcase on the bed, opened his drawers, and angrily tossed clothes in. "They want me outta here, I'm outta here," he muttered.

Michael appeared at his bedroom door. "You're really leaving," he said.

"How'd you get in?" Jeff asked.

"You don't exactly have a front door any-more . . . remember?"

"Oh, yeah, I forgot. So many bad things have happened I can't remember them all. But that's all gonna change — I'm leaving, and everything'll be roses and sunshine around here. That's what everybody wants, right?"

"Everybody's just scared, Jeff. That's all. Don't blame them."

"I blame them," Jeff said. "I blame them . . . and I blame myself. We're all guilty, Michael. Everybody's afraid of the magic words *confrontation* and *commitment*. I'm just as guilty as anybody else. I never stood up to anybody . . . until I got those powers. And they made me so strong that I didn't have any reason to be afraid. *That's* not bravery."

"You're being hard on yourself," Michael said.

"No I'm not," Jeff told him. "I'm being truthful. I've never been brave. And I've never been really committed to anything. Not Stacy, not my students, not this community. Stacy was right — the only thing I cared about was my music. And even there, I didn't give it my all. I didn't understand before: To really be a winner, you gotta . . . give up something."

Michael looked at the floor. Jeff threw another shirt into his suitcase.

*   *   *

Meanwhile . . .

On a rooftop across the street, Squirrel watched Jeff through binoculars. She put the binoculars down and ran across the roof to the top of the fire escape. She called down to the alley, "He's there."

Down in the alley, Simon turned to the Golden Lords and the Baby Lords. "Okay. Let's get started."

Goldilocks pulled out a cellular phone and said, "Okay. Roll 'em."

At that moment, four huge trucks, driven by Golden Lords, went into action. One parked sideways on Jeff's street, blocking it to the north; another blocked it to the south. The other two trucks parked on the cross street. Now, no traffic could get into Jeff's neighborhood, or out of it. Everything was blocked off except one alley.

Simon, Uzi, and Goldilocks came down this alley now, toward Jeff's building. When they got to the street, Simon saw a telephone pole. He stopped and thought a minute, then told Goldilocks, "Hold my calls."

Goldilocks grinned and shimmied up the pole. When he was at the top, he took out a pair of wire cutters and cut the telephone line. No telephone calls could get in or out of the neighborhood.

Up in his apartment, Jeff sat on the floor, face to face with Ellington. "Well, boy," Jeff said in his normal voice, "it was fun being able to really talk with you. I'm going to miss that. I just wish I could talk to you one last time. Just to say thank you."

Ellington licked Jeff's face. Jeff smiled and said, "Oh . . . thanks, Ellington."

Then he heard a voice from outside. He'd heard it before . . . it was the leader of the Golden Lords. "Meteor Man . . . Come on out, Meteor Man!"

Chapter 15

Jeff walked toward the door.

Michael grabbed his arm. "Jeff, you can't go down there. They'll kill you!"

"What can I do? Wait in here till they go away? Hide under the bed?"

"No, but . . ."

"I've got no choice," Jeff said. He walked out into the hall and down the stairs. Several neighbors cracked open their doors and watched him pass. Jeff saw Mr. Moses peer out with a pitiful expression, then close his door again. When he came to Mrs. Walker's door, Jeff paused. Then he kept going.

Mrs. Walker opened her door and came out into the hall. "Jeff . . . we're sorry."

Jeff looked back at her a moment. Then he continued down the stairs.

When he went outside, all the Golden Lords and Baby Lords were in the street. At the front of the group was Simon. He had on an expensive-looking black suit and had his hands on his hips.

Jeff walked down and stood in front of Simon.

Michael was watching from upstairs. He ran to Jeff's phone and tried to dial the police. But the phone was dead.

Looking Simon in the eye, Jeff raised his fists.

Simon began to laugh. "You know, brother, you got a lot of heart. Listen, man. I'm sorry about what we did to your neighborhood. No more of this, okay? Peace."

Simon extended his hand. Jeff just looked at it, confused. Was he being for real? He shouldn't trust him. Then again, maybe Simon realized what a horrible thing the Golden Lords had done. Maybe he *was* being for real.

Jeff clasped his hand and shook it.

Simon yanked him forward and butted heads with him. Jeff fell to his knees. Simon kicked him in the stomach.

* * *

Up in Jeff's apartment, Michael searched frantically until he found Jeff's address book. He stuck it in his pocket, then ran into the hall and up to the roof. He ran to the edge of the roof and climbed down the back fire escape to the alley. He ran until he found a pay phone; he pulled out Jeff's address book and called the leader of the Bloods.

Lying on the ground, Jeff heard his mother cry out, "Somebody help him!"

Simon took off his jacket and handed it to Uzi. "Get up," Simon ordered Jeff. "Don't you wanna play some more?"

Come on, Jeff told himself. Stand up. You can do it.

He stood shakily. Simon threw a punch. Jeff blocked it and threw a punch of his own, hitting Simon square in the mouth. Simon stumbled back, blood on his bottom lip.

Uzi and Goldilocks moved toward Jeff. "Leave him alone!" Simon yelled. "I don't need help."

Uzi and Goldilocks backed off.

Simon lunged at Jeff and grabbed him

147

around the waist. Jeff stumbled backward and landed painfully against the hood of a car. Simon backed up a step and aimed one of his boots at Jeff's face. Jeff jumped out of the way — and Simon kicked a huge dent in the car.

Jeff attacked. He threw several wild punches, missing with each one — and thinking, They make this look so easy on TV!

Finally, one of his punches caught Simon on his jaw. But Simon only looked madder. He threw two counterpunches, and Jeff fell to the ground.

In the alley, the only route that wasn't blocked off, a man walked unhurriedly, followed by three mutts. This was the man who had been present when Jeff was hit by the meteor. The man, whose name was Marvin, wore the same clothes he had worn that night. He had on stained pants, a moth-eaten gray coat, fingerless gloves, and a beaten-up porkpie hat. He carried a coffee can. Inside the can was a round, green, glowing object: the remains of the meteor. Marvin and his mutts wandered down the alley in the direction of Jeff's street.

Jeff, meanwhile, was not having an easy time. He was still on the ground, trying his best to dodge Simon's foot.

Nearby, Dre and Squirrel watched with frowns as Jeff kept getting kicked.

Finally, Jeff rolled over and got to his feet. But he'd only been standing a second when Simon hit him again, and he fell back down.

"Give up, Jeff! Stay down!" Mrs. Harris called from her window.

In the alley, Marvin heard someone running up behind him. He looked back and saw Michael, who was carrying a lead pipe. Michael shot past Marvin and the mutts, headed for the fight. He rounded a corner and saw Simon standing over Jeff. Michael clenched his teeth and ran straight for Simon with the pipe raised in the air. But Goldilocks saw him coming — and threw a kick that caught Michael in the pit of his stomach. He fell to the ground, gasping for air.

* * *

Jeff struggled to his feet one more time.

Simon looked amazed. "You want *more*?" he asked.

Jeff was practically seeing double, but he raised his fists and shouted, "Yeah . . . chump! Come on!"

With all his strength, he threw a punch at Simon — but it missed. Simon threw a punch which, unfortunately, did not miss. It caught Jeff on the chin. Jeff stumbled backward.

But this time, Jeff didn't fall. He caught his balance and then he charged Simon again. Growling with anger, Jeff threw punch after punch, and they connected. He caught Simon with a hook to the right cheek, another to the left cheek, and a jab to his ribs. He threw another left to Simon's face, followed by a right, followed by another left — and Simon, wearing a look of disbelief, fell to the ground.

This time, Jeff stood over Simon. "Come on, get up," he called down to him. "Don't you want to — "

At that moment, Goldilocks grabbed Michael's pipe and hit Jeff on the back of the neck. Jeff collapsed to the ground.

Simon climbed slowly to his feet and pulled out his pistol. He pointed it down at Jeff. Breathing hard, he said, "Any way you look at it, I still got you." His thumb drew back the hammer on the pistol. Jeff thought, It's over, and closed his eyes.

Up in the window, Mr. Moses threw something toward the street. It was an old, one-of-a-kind Billie Holliday record. It sailed through the air like a spaceship and caught Simon on the hand. His pistol fell to the ground.

Simon looked up angrily and saw Mr. Moses. Mr. Moses wore no toupee now; his bald head gleamed defiantly. "That'll cost you!" Simon shouted up at him. He bent down for his pistol.

But just before his hand could reach it, Squirrel kicked it away. Then Dre picked it up and threw it down the street.

Simon looked at them both, confused. "Are you crazy? Whose side are you on?" He turned and yelled out, "Golden Lords!"

Goldilocks, Uzi, and the other Lords pulled out their pistols and surrounded Jeff and Michael. The Baby Lords formed a circle around Squirrel and Dre.

Marvin and his mutts made it to the

street. Marvin saw what was happening. He stuck his hand inside the coffee can, rubbing the meteor. Then, with the same hand, he pointed at the Golden Lords. Suddenly, their pistols all flew out of their hands. Marvin continued to guide them with his finger, and the pistols took to the sky, like a flock of birds heading south for the winter.

Now, mayhem set in. The street began to look like a scene from a western movie. Fists flew in every direction. Jeff didn't understand a bit of what was going on; he only knew that he was still alive and suddenly seemed to have a fighting chance. He fought it out with the Golden Lords, punching, getting punched, and punching back again. Beside him, Michael was duking it out, too. Across from him, Dre and Squirrel tangled with the Baby Lords.

Then the neighbors got into the act. They took to the street and started swinging and throwing whatever they could get their hands on. Mrs. Harris had a twenty-pound sack of potatoes and hurled them at every blond head she saw. Mr. Reed, with his one good arm, was swinging a baseball bat. Mr.

Moses ran out with a stack of records and threw them like Frisbees.

Marvin barked to his mutts. The mutts charged toward the Golden Lords and bit like sharks.

Uzi called over to Goldilocks, "We was doin' so good! What happened?!"

Mrs. Harris aimed an especially large potato at Simon's head. But she missed, and the potato hit Marvin's coffee can instead. The meteor, now the size of a baseball, fell out. It rolled down the street, past the mutts and between people's legs.

Jeff saw it rolling toward him. His mouth fell open, and he stared at it.

Simon saw Jeff staring. Then he saw the meteor. And he figured it out.

Jeff and Simon ran toward the meteor at the same time.

Chapter 16

Jeff and Simon got to the meteor simultaneously. When they reached down for it, their shoulders rammed together. Jeff and Simon fell on the ground. The meteor stayed where it was.

Simon got on his feet first and lurched toward the glowing green prize. But Jeff dived at Simon, grabbing him around the waist before he could reach it. Simon fell on his back with Jeff on top of him. He punched Jeff in the ribs until Jeff rolled off. Then, as Simon got up and ran toward the meteor again, Jeff tripped him with his foot — and Simon fell to the ground once more.

Like an infantry soldier, Simon crawled on his belly toward the meteor. Jeff crawled after him. When Simon was about to reach out and touch the meteor, Jeff grabbed him by the ankles and dragged him backward. Then Jeff ran toward the meteor himself. But Simon got to his feet and hit Jeff with a body block. Jeff stumbled, but regained his balance. Both of them ran toward it again.

Goldilocks saw what was happening and ran for the meteor himself. Michael took off after Goldilocks. Goldilocks reached down for the prize; his hands were so close that they were bathed in green light. But Michael grabbed his waist and pulled him backward. Desperately, Goldilocks reached for the meteor with his foot. He ended up kicking it, and it rolled toward . . .

Simon. He now had both hands on it and was grinning like a maniac. But then Jeff grabbed it, too. They each held it tightly with both hands.

"I can feel the power from this thing!" Simon said. "You got a lot of heart, man . . . join me. We can rule together!"

"Never!" Jeff told him.

"All right, then," Simon grunted. "You just blew your last chance to get out of this alive!"

As the power from the meteor was channeled into both their bodies, the meteor itself got smaller. When it disappeared altogether, there was a blinding flash and a deafening explosion. Jeff was hurled backward twenty feet and came to a stop against the side of a car. Simon was tossed in the opposite direction and landed on the sidewalk.

Simon stood up and shook his head, clearing it. Then something confused him. Marvin's mutts attacked Goldilocks and Uzi, and as they barked, Simon could swear they were saying words.

"Bite him good!" one mutt was saying.

"No sweat! I'm half pit bull!" another answered.

On the other side of the street, Jeff was placing his hands on his swollen face and his aching ribs. Both were instantly healed. He heard the mutts barking, and understood what they were saying, and smiled to himself. He glanced toward the battle that was taking place between the neighbors and the Golden Lords. He could see the underwear of everyone involved. His X-ray vision was back. "Yeah!" Jeff shouted. He was Meteor Man again!

But he wasn't alone.

Jeff looked up, and a van was speeding toward him. Only it had no driver — it was being pushed by Simon!

Jeff dived out of the way right before the van crashed into the parked car. The van, it turned out, belonged to a plumber — and when it crashed, about fifty metal pipes rolled out and into the street.

Simon stood in the middle of the street with his fists raised above his head. "Yeaaaahhh!" he shouted. "Now *this* is what I call feeling *strong*!"

Jeff watched him and thought, This is what I call feeling *scared*.

Simon went over to a NO PARKING sign and pulled it out of the concrete. He hurled it like a spear at Jeff.

Marvin pointed his finger at the sign to try and stop it. But he was hit over the head from behind by Goldilocks. Marvin fell to the ground. His mutts came running over.

Meanwhile, Jeff dodged the sign, just in time. Simon then ripped a parking meter out of the ground. Jeff ran to a car and tore the door off. Simon threw the parking meter at Jeff; Jeff blocked it with the car door.

Simon picked up a pipe from the ground and charged Jeff. The pipe became like a sword, and the car door like a shield. Simon swung the pipe at Jeff's face, chest, and stomach; but Jeff blocked it every time. The *bang, bang, bang* could be heard all over the neighborhood.

Then Uzi and another Golden Lord grabbed pipes and sneaked up behind Jeff. "Mr. Reed, behind you!" Squirrel shouted.

Jeff turned around just in time to block the blows from the pipes. More Lords ran over with pipes. Jeff leapt onto the hood of a car. Still holding the car door, he used it to protect himself against pipe thrusts from all directions. *Bang*, he blocked one from the left; *clank*, he stopped one on the right.

Viewed from above, the street now resembled a scene from the days of King Arthur. Neighbors and Golden Lords grabbed pipes and battled with them as if they were swords. With his good arm, Mr. Reed swung with all his might. Mr. Moses had now forgotten his fear. He had run out of records to throw, but he got hold of a pipe and wielded it with the energy of a man half his age. The younger neighbors got into the act, too.

Dre and Squirrel were back-to-back, trading punches with the Baby Lords.

Meanwhile, Jeff was still on the hood of the car, fending off pipes with the door. A tiny smile appeared on his face; he was starting to enjoy this a little. He pointed a finger at one of his attackers, who then went sailing backward as if he'd been catapulted. Jeff pointed at another Lord. This one began doing involuntary handsprings down the street, yelling the whole way.

But now there was Simon to deal with. With a scowl on his face, he ran up and kicked the car Jeff was standing on. Jeff flipped over forward, landing on his back on the ground.

When he got up, Simon sent a fist crashing into his jaw, then punched him in the stomach. Jeff doubled over in pain. Simon hit him once more, finally knocking Jeff to the ground.

Simon picked up the now helpless Jeff and raised him over his head. "This is what I think of your Meteor Man!" Simon yelled to the neighborhood as he tossed Jeff through the air. Neighbors and Golden Lords alike ducked as Jeff passed overhead.

At the end of the block was a mobile library truck. Jeff sailed in one end and out the other — crashing through the windshield and bursting out the back door along with a pile of books.

As he struggled to get up, Jeff's hand fell on the topmost book. The title of the book was *Bruce Lee's Master Karate Techniques*. A green spark danced between the book and Jeff's hand.

"Ah-ha," Jeff said.

Michael yelled at him, "Thirty seconds, Jeff! Go!"

Simon came running toward Jeff. He threw a punch — but Jeff blocked it with his forearm, then hit him with three fast kicks. Simon stumbled backward in shock.

Michael looked at his watch and yelled, "Twenty-five seconds!"

More Lords rushed at Jeff. Jeff sent them all reeling back: one from a chop, another from a roundhouse kick.

"Seventeen seconds!"

Jeff ran at Simon and unleashed several punches, kicks, and chops. With each one,

Simon yelled out in pain. He tried throwing punches of his own, but Jeff just blocked them and resumed the attack.

Simon spun backward.

"Ten seconds!"

Some Lords began throwing pipes at Jeff. Jeff aimed his eye lasers at the pipes, melting them in midair. Puddles of hot liquid metal formed on the ground.

Jeff turned back to Simon. But then, all at once, he forgot what he was about to do. The thirty seconds were up — and Jeff's knowledge of karate passed right out of his mind. What's more, his arms and legs were now exhausted from throwing all the chops and kicks.

And Simon was still standing.

Chapter 17

Jeff ran back toward the pile of books. He grabbed the one on top, and another green spark flew. But something was wrong. Jeff looked at the cover of the book. This wasn't *Bruce Lee's Master Karate Techniques*. It was *Ballet Made Simple*.

But Simon didn't know this. As Jeff tossed the book away, Simon ran up and grabbed it with both hands. More green sparks flew.

Simon dropped the book. For a moment, he and Jeff looked at each other confused.

Then they ran toward each other on tip-toe. When they were a foot apart, they leapt gracefully into the air, sailing past each other with their hands over their heads.

Michael looked at his watch. "Twenty-six seconds of *Swan Lake* left," he said.

Goldilocks and Uzi looked at each other strangely.

Jeff tried to run toward Simon. Instead, he leaned over sideways, and kind of . . . *pranced* toward him. Simon came at Jeff the same way. When they met, they exchanged dirty looks, then twirled past each other.

"Seventeen seconds. Baryshnikov, eat your heart out."

With his forearm resting on his forehead, and his other arm pointing out behind him, Jeff danced once more toward Simon. Meanwhile, Simon had one leg up on a car, doing stretching exercises.

"Nine seconds until the curtain falls," Michael said.

Now, Jeff and Simon ran all over the street, spinning and twirling. Finally, each took a running leap. When they landed, they each took a bow. The thirty seconds were up.

"Bravo!" Michael said. "I mean . . . thank goodness that's over!"

Simon rushed at Jeff, showering him with punches. Jeff was too tired to fight back — almost too tired to block the punches. He took blows to his face, ribs, and stomach, finally falling to the ground.

Simon walked over to where a huge trash Dumpster sat. He picked it up and came back over toward Jeff, who was so dazed he didn't know what was happening.

Then Ellington ran out into the street. "Jeff!" he barked. "Watch out!"

Simon turned toward Ellington with the Dumpster.

Jeff turned his head and saw what was about to happen. With his last bit of energy, he hollered, "Nooooo!"

Simon viciously hurled the Dumpster at Ellington. The dog ran — but not fast enough. The Dumpster pinned him to the ground.

Simon picked Jeff up. He tossed him ten feet off the ground. As Jeff was coming down again, Simon yelled "Extra point!" and kicked him like a football. Jeff went sailing up into the air, landing with a sickening thud on the roof of his apartment building.

Simon now stood in the middle of the

street with his fists raised above his head. He shouted to the whole neighborhood: "Now the world will do as I say!" He turned to Uzi and said, "Shoot me!"

Uzi was confused. "What?"

"You heard me! Shoot me!"

Goldilocks opened the trunk of a car and pulled out a gun. He tossed it to Uzi. Uzi, with an "I hope you know what you're doing" expression, pointed the gun at Simon.

"Shoot me now!"

He fired. The bullet bounced off Simon's chest.

"More! More!"

Uzi fired away. Simon began doing a dance. As he did, the bullets bounced off him like rubber bands. Finally, Uzi ran out of bullets. Simon grinned from ear to ear. "I will rule this planet!" he shouted. "I want to meet with all the top world leaders . . . the president . . . Boris Yeltsin . . . Al Sharpton!"

On the roof . . .

Jeff lay flat on his stomach. His vision was blurred; he had never ached so much in his life. He felt as if his body had been taken apart and put back together the wrong way. Like a figure moving in slow motion, he crawled to the edge of the roof and looked down at the street. Simon was standing triumphant. He looked unstoppable. If *I* have to stop him, then I guess he *is* unstoppable, Jeff thought.

Then he saw something else. His neighbors, Dre and Squirrel, were still fighting. Even though things looked hopeless, they were seeing it through to the end.

Well, Jeff thought, if they can, so can I. With a loud groan, he stood up and went to the door that led to the roof. He climbed down and went to his apartment. In his bedroom was his Meteor Man uniform. "Sometimes it helps if you *look* the part," he said as he pulled on his tights.

In the street, Dre was holding his own against two Baby Lords. Squirrel, backed into a corner by two Golden Lords, was holding them at bay with a pipe. A victorious Mr. Moses was chasing his opponent down the street with *two* pipes, clobbering him on the shoulders. Michael traded punches with Goldilocks. Mrs. Walker tried to help Ellington, who was still trapped under the Dumpster, wheezing and kicking weakly.

Uzi pointed upward. "Simon! Look!"

Simon looked. Standing on the roof, with his feet spread apart, his fists resting on his waist, and his cape blowing in the wind, was . . .

"Meteor Man!"

Chapter 18

As if he were jumping into a swimming pool, Meteor Man dived off the roof. He flew down to the street and made a smooth landing in front of Simon.

Simon looked as if he were seeing someone rise from the grave. "You changed your clothes," was all he could say.

"The show's over," Meteor Man said.

"Says who?"

"Says . . . me!"

Meteor Man flew at Simon and threw a right cross, then a left, turning Simon's head with each punch. Simon stumbled back, dazed. With dizzying speed, Meteor Man flew in circles around him, stunning him with punch after punch. Finally, Simon hit the ground. He was out cold.

Meteor Man stood over Simon and grabbed his hands. Squeezing them hard, he drained all the meteor energy from Simon — and drew it into himself. Now, Meteor Man's powers were his own again!

He flew to the plumber's van and grabbed a long orange extension cord. He then flew in circles around Goldilocks, Uzi, and the other Golden Lords, and in less than a minute they were all bound up together.

Next, the Baby Lords. Two of them had finally subdued Dre; they were kneeling over him while the others stood around shouting.

Meteor Man walked up behind them and cleared his throat loudly. The Baby Lords turned toward him and raised their fists, ready to fight.

Meteor Man chuckled and said, "All that heart gone to waste." He flew in circles around the Baby Lords. As he passed each one, he pulled off parts of their outfits — jackets, shirts, shoes, socks. When Meteor Man came to a stop, he held in his arms what looked like a huge pile of laundry. The

Baby Lords were still standing in a circle, dizzy and half-dressed.

Then Meteor Man started flying around them again. This time, he tied all the clothes together as he flew — and wrapped them around the Baby Lords. When he came to a stop, the Baby Lords were bound together by a rope made from their own clothes.

"That ought to hold you until the juvenile authorities get here," Meteor Man said.

Then he looked to his left. A group of his neighbors were huddled around the trash Dumpster. Meteor Man walked over. Ellington had been pulled from underneath the Dumpster, but was lying in the street, hardly moving. Mr. and Mrs. Reed kneeled over him, petting him.

Michael looked at Jeff sadly. "Jeff, I don't think he's . . ."

Jeff squeezed in and knelt down beside his dog. Ellington's head turned slightly toward Jeff.

Jeff petted his dog and barked, "How you doin' there, boy?"

Wheezing, Ellington barked weakly, "Did we win?"

Jeff nodded.

Ellington tried to bark, but couldn't.

Jeff used his X-ray vision to see inside Ellington's body. The damage, it seemed, was a crushed rib cage. Jeff placed his hand gently on Ellington's side and barked, "You're not going anywhere."

Jeff concentrated, trying to use his power to heal. But Ellington didn't seem to respond. Jeff tried to look inside Ellington's body again — but this time, he couldn't see. His powers were disappearing again. Jeff looked at Ellington, who was still hardly moving. Tears filled Jeff's eyes.

Then a pair of large, crusty hands reached down toward Ellington. Jeff looked up to see Marvin.

"Let's see what we can do here," Marvin said.

As his hands touched Ellington's sides, they glowed green. Ellington began to stir a little. Jeff placed his hands gently on his dog. With the last of his powers, he helped Marvin to heal him. In a matter of seconds, Ellington was up again and licking Jeff's face.

"Heyyy, boy!" Jeff shouted, gleeful. He

hugged his dog. The neighbors all cheered. Michael clapped Marvin on the shoulder and shook his hand.

But it wasn't quite time for celebration. Mr. Reed pointed down the street and said, "Look!"

Everyone's head turned. Mr. Reed was pointing toward one of the huge trucks that blocked the street. Men in black clothes were stepping around both ends of the truck and walking toward Jeff and his neighbors. Each of the men held a pistol.

The last man to emerge from behind the truck was Alexander Byers.

Byers walked up to Jeff wearing a smile that wasn't really a smile. "You would have to be Meteor Man," he said.

"Who are you?" Jeff asked.

"The man who's about to oversee your execution." Byers glanced at the Golden Lords, who were all tied up, and at Simon, who was still out cold on the ground. "Something told me this was too important to leave to underlings. So while the Golden Lords were following you around, I had my men follow *them* around. Gentlemen . . ."

When Byers said "Gentlemen," the men dressed in black pointed their guns at Jeff.

Jeff tried aiming his eye-lasers at the guns. But nothing happened.

"Any last words?" Byers asked Jeff.

Jeff just stared at him.

"Well, if not," Byers said, "I have some last words for you. *Have a nice trip!*"

The next second, a voice behind Jeff shouted, "His trip's just been canceled. Maybe you and your men want to take it?"

Everyone turned around. Snake, Poison, and two more Crips and Bloods stood in the street.

"Where . . . how . . . ?" Jeff asked.

"I called them," Michael said.

"You don't scare me," Byers replied.

"Oh, no?" Snake said. He whistled loudly. Another hundred Bloods and Crips appeared. They lined the sidewalks and the rooftops, holding uzis, shotguns, and pistols.

Byers cleared his throat and muttered, "Well, on second thought . . ." He and his hit men backed up slowly and quietly and disappeared again behind the truck.

Jeff turned to Snake and Poison. "I don't know how to thank you guys."

"Anytime you need us, call," Snake said. He and Poison and the rest of the Bloods and Crips disappeared into the night.

Then came the sound of police sirens. The trucks were towed away, letting traffic into the neighborhood again. Then more policemen arrived and began questioning the neighbors.

Mrs. Walker ran up to one of the policemen. "I was a victim of a crime last week, and I was afraid to come forward. But now I want to press charges against Simon Hawkins."

Mrs. Harris pulled a thin branch from a tree and walked over to where the Baby Lords were tied up. She stood in front of them a moment, looking enraged. Then she began circling them almost as fast as Meteor Man and hitting them with the switch. The Baby Lords squirmed and shouted.

"What you need is an old-fashioned spanking," Mrs. Harris said. "I don't know who your mommas and daddies are, but I'm treating you like my own!"

When she was done she picked up one of the Baby Lords's portable phones and dialed. "Girl, we had some excitement around here to*night*. And I think I just met a new man," she said, gazing at Mr. Moses.

Mr. Moses batted his eyes back at her, his bald head gleaming.

Jeff ducked inside his apartment building and changed into jeans and a sweatshirt. When he came back out, he walked up to Dre and Squirrel. Dre was sitting on the ground, and Squirrel was wiping Dre's bloody nose with a handkerchief.

Jeff knelt down beside them. "Listen . . . I really have to thank you two. You really came through for me."

"You welcome, Mr. Reed," Dre and Squirrel said quietly.

"It looks to me like the Golden Lords are finished. Who are you two going to hang around with now?"

Dre and Squirrel shrugged.

"Your parents and your teachers aren't perfect. But you should give them a chance," Jeff said. "They want to do what's best for you. Not like the gangs."

"We'll have to see," Squirrel answered.

Maybe that's all I can ask for right now, Jeff thought. He grabbed Ellington and went back inside his apartment.

He watched the scene in the street from his window. The police were writing down testimonies from Mrs. Walker and Jeff's father. The Golden Lords were being loaded into a police wagon. Simon, looking dazed, was being escorted to a patrol car. Michael was talking with two young women from the neighborhood.

The scene, Jeff thought, looked very . . . hopeful.

Chapter 19

At school the next morning, Jeff was walking down the hall when he saw Michael coming toward him. His arm was in a sling.

"Hey, man, what happened?" Jeff said.

"Well, somewhere in the middle of all that scrapping with the Golden Lords, I sprained my elbow."

"Oh, man."

"Hey, don't worry. The doctor says it'll heal in no time. And in the meantime, I get a lot of sympathy from the ladies. Check you later!"

Jeff smiled and shook his head. Then he walked into Mrs. Laws's office.

Mrs. Laws was sitting behind her desk

going over some papers. She glanced up over the tops of her glasses and said, "Yes? May I help you, Mr. Reed?"

"I just wanted to tell you something," Jeff said.

"Well, go ahead. Tell me!"

Jeff sighed. "Ever since I've been here, you've shot down my ideas. That's okay — maybe I wasn't totally committed to the kids before. But that's all different now. I just came by to say it's a new game."

Mrs. Laws smiled. "It's a new game."

"And one more thing," Jeff said. "I'm doing 'My Country 'Tis of Thee' my way, Warden."

Mrs. Laws stopped smiling. "What did you call me?"

"I said 'Warden,' Warden."

Jeff left. When he passed through the outer office, Michael was there. He and a small group of people were standing around a TV set. Michael waved Jeff over.

"What's going on?"

Michael pointed to the screen. Taking a closer look, Jeff realized a press conference was going on in his neighborhood. On the screen were Mr. and Mrs. Reed, Mr.

Moses, Mrs. Harris — and Marvin, who was wearing a new suit.

Mrs. Walker was speaking. "We, the people of the southeast community, want to let the gangs and the drug dealers know we are cleaning up our streets. We will videotape drug deals and write down license plate numbers. We are going to patrol our streets every night — adults, teenagers, and senior citizens. So when you see this . . ." Everyone on camera pulled out green caps with METEOR PATROL on the front. "Know that we are watching you!"

Jeff smiled at Michael and then left the office. Out in the hall, the first thing he saw was . . . his bass! It had a red ribbon around it. Next to it, holding it up, were Dre and Squirrel.

"We thought maybe you could use this," Squirrel said.

"You two . . ." Jeff said. "Thank you, Dre. Squirrel."

Squirrel smiled shyly and said, "Mr. Reed, could you call me Monique? That's my real name."

"You got it . . . Monique."

"We been talkin', Mr. Reed," Dre said.

"I was thinking — I wanna be a scientist. I'm smart enough. I think I can do it."

"And I really want to work on my singing," Monique said. "If I keep it up, I could make a record one day. Then, maybe later, I could run for president! Well, we have to get to class. See you later, Mr. Reed!"

Jeff waved good-bye to them. Then he looked way down at the other end of the hall and saw Stacy. He took off running after her. He caught up to her, almost out of breath, and said, "Stacy, can I talk to you for a minute?"

"Go right ahead," Stacy said.

"Those, um . . . those panty hose you saw in my bathroom? The gray ones? Those were mine."

Stacy laughed coldly. Jeff felt a chill go through him. "Right," Stacy said.

"I'm telling the truth. It's a long story. Can we talk about it over dinner? I know I've been stupid in the past — chasing rainbows. But for some reason, at the end of the rainbow I always see . . . your face."

Stacy seemed to be caught offguard, as if this were the last thing she expected to hear. Her face began to soften a little.

Then, all at once, she broke into a smile. "You really mean that?"

"Yeah."

Michael passed by. He saw Stacy, and winked at Jeff.

"You seem different," Stacy said. "Is something going on you're not telling me about?"

Jeff cleared his throat. "Well. I guess you've been hearing the news stories about a guy who . . . *flies*, and . . . well, the thing is — "

Suddenly, Michael was beside them. "Excuse me, Stacy. I'm sorry, Jeff. I have to talk to you for a second."

"Michael, I'm talking . . ."

"This is important!" Michael said.

"Well," Stacy said. "I'll see you later, Jeff. You can finish your explanation then. It sounded interesting."

Michael pulled Jeff by the arm. When they were out of anyone's earshot, Michael said, "Don't tell anyone you were ever Meteor Man."

"Why?"

"Because, look what I just got in the mail."

Michael reached into the pocket of his lab coat and pulled out a magazine called *Science Today*. On its cover was a huge green meteor sitting in the middle of the Arizona desert.

"The meteor," Jeff said. "So?"

"The meteor landed the same day you were hit!" Michael answered.

Jeff thought a second. If there was another piece of the meteor, and he could get to it . . . "But, Michael, after all this time, won't the meteor's energy be gone?"

"Look at the picture," Michael said. "The meteor has some kind of shell around it. The true energy source is at the core. If you chip away that shell, apply a little heat, Jefferson Reed is once again . . ."

"Meteor Man!" Jeff said. He and Michael slapped a high-five.

"We got to get to Arizona quick!" Jeff said.

"Jeff, if this works out, I want to fight crime with you."

"Michael, it's too dangerous."

"I don't care!" Michael said. "I want to fight crime with you. Side by side. I want superpowers, too!" He stroked his chin a second. "Hmmm . . . Meteor Man and

Comet Boy. *Nah,* I don't want nobody calling me 'boy.' Maybe Meteor Man and Chocolate Thunder."

"Michael . . ."

"Meteor Man and the Flying Wonder?"

"Michael!"

"Just something to think about."